HER EMERALD SHIELD

A GUARDIANS OF CAMELOT PORTAL FANTASY NOVEL

SARAH BIGLOW

For information contact; www.sarah-biglow.com

Edited by: Alecia Goodman, Under Wraps Publishing Services

Cover Design by: Deranged Doctor Design

Interior Art by: Therena Carlin

ISBN: 978-1-955988-43-8

10 9 8 7 6 5 4 3 2 1

 Created with Vellum

FROM THE AUTHOR

Special Thanks to:

Victoria Psomiadis, Ryan Scott James, Brian Grimes, Anonymous Reader, maileguy, Rosie Pease, Samantha Newberry, Tanya Young, Heiko Koenig, Yara Dijkstra, Samantha Ghormley, GhostCat, pjk, Jackie Kripas, Elizabeth W., Ayl, Matthew Walker, Chris Clayton, Francesco Tehrani, Stacy Ward, Catherine McP., Mono, Emily Welsby, Sue Frecker, Diane Hansebout, Lavar, Anna McCluskey, Vicki Hsu, Molly Zenk, Lorenzo, Michael W. Kerr, Scott Casey, Kathryn, Bonniejean Boettecher, Katherine Malloy, Melissa Showers, Gerald P. McDaniel, Finley Ymir, Niels Starfari, Stephen Ballentine, StarbuckApolloFemshepKaidanAliCole,, Danae, Susanna, PippiMD, Isaac Dansicker, Steven Byrd, Robin Hill, John Idlor, Nicola Thompson, Stacy Shuda, Adam Brooks, Courtney Arnold, Margaret St. John, Molly J. Stanton, Cathy McLoughlin, Billye Herndon, Justise Briones, Amanda, Alexandra Corrsin, Maria Mejia, Josefine Bällsten, Vanessa Goodwin, Jade Feinics, and Karen Bulgarelli.

CHAPTER
ONE

My head still spun an hour after Taron had dropped the dragon-shaped bomb on us that the arseholes who'd crippled our communications were not in fact the Seelies. I sat in my mother's private chambers, head in my hands trying to will the throbbing to subside. I sensed Emerys' magic from across the room wrap itself around me, easing the ache and I let out a soft sigh of relief.

"Morgan." My mother's voice was gentle as it called from across the room.

I forced myself to look up. "This is mental. It doesn't make sense."

Her lips pressed into a noncommittal line. "As you've seen, those we believe to be enemies can turn out to be our fiercest allies. Wouldn't you say that about Nim?"

I nodded mutely.

"Then it stands to reason that the opposite is also true."

"But what would they gain from taking both us and Uther offline?"

"Misinformation and chaos," Emerys answered from the doorway. "Allowing us to believe the other was responsible, the true architects likely hoped we would go to war and plunge the region into disarray in the process."

I looked at my mother. "Be straight with me. How close were we to that really becoming a reality?"

She wouldn't meet my gaze, which was an answer in itself. "We were preparing to find a way to activate our military with the communications still down."

"Just defensively though, right?"

She gave a slight shake of her head in the negative. "I know this is a lot for you to take in and understand. This is not the world you were raised in. If you had been, you'd understand that sometimes you have to act offensively to protect the people under your care."

"I'm the last person who would want to defend the Seelies, but it just feels wrong," I said.

"These types of decisions are always difficult, no matter the circumstances," Emerys noted and moved to stand beside me. "But the important thing to know is those actions do not need to be taken now. Peace can remain."

"You really think Uther is going to come shake our hands and sign the peace treaty if we tell him, oh it wasn't us ... it was some arsehole dragons fucking with us all?"

"I think we'd put it more delicately than that. But I think if we offer to share the technology you and your new friend brought back that restored access to our systems with him, he may be inclined to reconsider the treaty," my mother answered.

"Speaking of, I've spoken with the council, and they think you need to make a public statement, assuring the kingdom that all is well. No doubt rumors managed to swirl even without normal methods of communication."

"I think they're right." My mother stood and offered me her hand. "I want you by my side when I address everyone."

"Me, why?"

"You are the rightful heir to this kingdom,

Morgan. Those in the castle may have more easily accepted your role, but many in the kingdom require further proof, and reassurance. The more they can see you, the better."

I didn't like the idea of being paraded around, but she had a point. Aside from my entry in the tournament and the very public ousting of Arthur as both its champion and the rightful heir to Camelot's crown, my people hadn't gotten to know me. And with the frequent trips I'd taken through the barrier back to London and America, there hadn't been much time to let them get acquainted.

"Should we do something more, like I don't know ... an interview or something?"

"When everything has calmed down, I think that's an excellent idea," my mother answered and pulled me to my feet. "For now though, we need to reassure our people that we are back in control."

As I followed her out of the room, Emerys fell into step beside me. "Our new acquaintance is getting settled in. I asked Julayne and Gethin to look after her."

"Thanks." I knew I should have taken care of Avery myself, but I'd just been too thrown off kilter to be of much use to anyone. As we moved through the corridors back to the Council Chamber to go over the high points of my mother's speech, I couldn't help but scan faces for Taron.

"Your dragon prince has returned to his kingdom," Emery said, as if reading my mind.

"Guess I'll have to go track him down." He clearly knew more than he'd let on about the dragons who'd nearly ignited a war.

"One thing at a time," she said.

She stopped at the doorway to the chamber and when I fixed her with a quizzical look, she shrugged. "I have other duties to attend to. Do try to pay attention in there. Politics may look uninteresting at first blush, but one day it will be you making these decisions."

"Understood."

Following my mother inside, one of the security officers pulled the door shut behind me. The space was unchanged from its layout an hour ago and yet it felt even more chaotic. I did my best to parse as people raised different issues they thought my mother needed to address. After about ten minutes of back and forth, I found myself tuning it all out.

Maybe I wasn't cut out for this after all. It wasn't as if anyone was asking for my opinion on the matters; not that I had one to give. Someone tapped my shoulder, startling me out of my daze. I turned to find Shunae seated beside me.

"You look overwhelmed."

"Well, it's a bit much. I don't know how you do this all the time."

"I'm really good at arguing," she said with a smile. "And I've had a lot of time to practice, too."

"Do you think Uther will accept our help and agree to the treaty after all of this?"

"I think Uther is a man who likes to be in control and the fact we currently have the upper hand is going to unnerve him. But I also know he hates being seen as weak. My guess is he'll privately accept our help, but publicly decry any knowledge that we gave them the solution."

"But he wants Camelot. That's clear from everything he's done. So, why not still blame us and attack?"

"Because once we show proof it wasn't us, he knows that we can combat any propaganda he puts out there. He wants to take us on in his own way, on his own terms."

"Oddly, I find that sort of comforting."

"The more time you spend around Seelies, the more you understand it's just all about power for them. The key is making them think they've got it, even when you're really the one with the upper hand. They respect that sort of thing."

"Can I ask you something?"

"You are technically my superior, so if you ask me something, I'm obligated to answer."

"You grew up with Arthur, did you ever suspect something was off about him?"

"I didn't come into the Queen's service until we were both adults. And at that point, I guess he'd become skilled at hiding who he really was."

"But how did he manage to fool everyone during the time he was a baby?"

"That's something we've all been trying to figure out. From what we can guess, Uther placed some sort of concealment spell on him. How he managed to keep it going over time without access to him, we don't know."

"Morgan, we're ready," my mother called, interrupting our conversation.

"Guess I've got to go look pretty and stand for the camera, so people remember I exist," I said.

"You're more than just a pretty face. I've seen you fight before. People would do well to remember that you are a fierce warrior."

I let Shunae's words buoy my spirits as we moved to the front steps of the castle inside the courtyard. I could see the stone where Excalibur had sat three decades waiting for me. A camera crew assembled not far from us, and I was reminded of the announcement my mother had made not long after the tournament ended, crowning me the winner. I felt just as awkward now as I did then. I let the court staff primp and prod me to make my appearance camera ready and usher me to a spot to my mother's left. I was grateful they hadn't forced me to change out of my jeans and boots. However, they'd insisted I change into a dark blue blouse with silver piping that billowed out over my arms.

Focused on my conversation with Shunae, I hadn't noticed my mother don her crown or a floor-length long sleeved dark blue gown, but the metallic glint caught my eye as the sun struck her face. She looked regal even as she stood there, studying some briefly scribbled notes. I could only hope that one day I might have her poise as the camera man counted down from five. She stowed her notes and stepped up to the podium they'd staged for the address.

"Citizens of Camelot, I know the last few days have been filled with confusion and uncertainty as we faced severe technological challenges. But I want to assure you that all is well. Camelot is safe. Our network and communications systems are working as they should." She took a moment and looked from one side of the assembled camera crew to the other, no doubt giving the effect that she was looking at the people watching on the other end. "I know many of you have questions about how such an affront on our kingdom could happen and what we are doing to protect you. Those are valid concerns, and we are still working to assess the full extent of the damage. I assure you we will give you the answers you seek as soon as we have them."

I did my best not to fidget as I stood in silence. Shunae was right that the people needed to see me, but I suddenly felt like I was under a microscope, and everyone was silently judging me. What good was I just standing motionless when I could be doing ... *something*.

My mother's voice pulled me out of my mental spiral. "To our neighbors, we are grateful for your support in our time of trepidation. Without you we could not have come through this as we have." She nodded in my direction. "And I must thank my daughter, Morgan, for her own tireless efforts in seeking creative solutions to address our kingdom's technology problems."

That made me stand straighter.

"Because of her, we have come into possession of key information that will help safeguard us in the future." Her face shifted from conciliatory to a more neutral expression. "To those who would call us enemies, we hope this message can reach you. Know that if you have been similarly affected, we will do all we can to share what we have learned, so that you can recover, too."

With that, the light on the camera went dark and the lights behind it turned off. I exhaled when the cinematographer gave a thumb's up to signal that we were no longer recording.

"You didn't have to say anything about me," I said.

"The people need to know that you, the rightful heir, have their best interests in mind and that you are working to secure their future."

"But doesn't that kind of tip off these dragon nutters that we know what they've done?"

"The fact we were able to disseminate information like this should tell them we've regained control," she replied. "And I highly suspect your friend's magic already warned them that they were no longer in control."

"How much do you know about these Inferno blokes?"

"Woefully little I'm afraid. They aren't something that's come up during my reign."

Well, that needed to change. "I got the feeling Taron knew more than just what their symbol stood for."

My mother stopped walking mid-pace and pivoted to face me. We stood in the corridor alone and I watched as she schooled her expression into something that resembled the look Nim got whenever I brought a new boyfriend around. "I understand your attraction to him, but you need to tread carefully."

"He's our ally," I retorted.

"That is true. The dragons have been historically benevolent when it comes to our kingdom and that isn't something I expect to change given the leadership they have rising in the ranks. But whether you like it or not, the people you associate with are under scrutiny. And that goes doubly so for the people you choose to associate with privately."

"Just talking with him can't possibly cause a diplomatic incident."

She gave me a small smile. "No, but arriving in his arms from who knows where does raise eyebrows."

"Once. That happened one bloody time and it was time sensitive."

"It wasn't the first time he's been spotted."

"Look, I promise I'll be careful. I just want to see what he knows about these Syndicate arseholes. Maybe it's something we could use to stop them from hacking us again or doing whatever chaotic bullshit they've got planned next."

"You are a grown woman and I know nothing I say will stop you from seeing him. Morgan ... Just, be mindful." She looked as if she had more to say, but she remained silent.

"Right, I'm going to see how Avery is getting on and find out as much as I can about these psychos. I promise to try to find something we can use."

"From the moment I saw you in the tournament, I knew you were a woman born of determination. I have no doubt you will keep our people safe."

I stood awkwardly for a moment before leaving her in the corridor as I went in search of my friends. There was no way that Gethin or Jules would let me do this solo. Besides, I was beginning to suspect, none of this was meant to be something I accomplished alone. As I traversed around the castle, I retrieved my phone and scrolled through my contacts until I found Taron's number. I stopped walking long enough to send him a message.

Uh, hi, it's Morgan. We need to talk. I think we both know you've got more info on the Syndicate than you let on before and this affects both our kingdoms. Can you come to the castle? I know it's not our usual meeting spot, but this feels like it ought to be more official.

I didn't have to wait long for a reply.

I will be there within an hour.

The length of time for his arrival seemed suspiciously long, but I let it go. The time would allow me time to fill everyone else in and start to formulate a plan of attack. I wound my way through the upper corridors to the bedrooms and followed the sound of Gethin's voice until I ended up in the doorway of Avery's room. He and Avery stood in front of a desk with a laptop perched haphazardly on one edge.

"Everything okay in here?"

Gethin jolted upright at the sound of my voice, nearly knocking the computer to the floor. Avery righted it deftly with one hand.

"Yeah, everything's fine," he replied, adjusting his glasses.

"Grand, because we're about to go digging into some ancient evil dragons."

TWO

My words caught Gethin's attention instantly. He straightened and resettled his glasses on his nose for a second time.

"Evil dragons? What did I miss?"

Avery took a step forward. "Apparently, the people ... uh, beings responsible for taking down your system were dragons. I admit it's a lot to wrap my head around, too."

"Not something I've heard of before."

"Don't worry, I've got an expert on the way to assist," I said, trying not to betray my excitement at seeing Taron again.

Avery flashed me a knowing smile that she quickly hid behind a fake cough when Gethin turned to look at her. She was going to keep my secret for now at least. I glanced around the space. "Where's Jules? I thought she was helping you."

"Oh, Jules had to go check on some things and then Gethin popped by to make sure I was getting settled in," Avery explained.

I didn't like that my best friend had up and vanished on me when I could use her researching skills. Though I had a feeling the three of us plus Taron would be on the crowded side. "I caught the tail end of the queen's address," Gethin noted, pointing to Avery's closed laptop. "It was awfully nice of her to acknowledge your efforts."

"As everyone keeps reminding me, the people don't really know the true heir. So, they're trying to find ways to get me in front of the populace. I have to admit I'm not a fan, but I doubt there's anything I can do about it."

"They aren't wrong," he said. "I mean, sure, everyone's seen you fight and knows you can hold your own in a battle, but that's just one side of you. They need to know the woman behind the spells."

"I get it, trust me. And saving the kingdom from the brink of an unnecessary war likely goes a long way toward showing them that I have their best interests in mind. But making sure these ancient prats can't take another whack at us is better."

"How do you know they're ancient?" Avery interrupted.

"Because from my limited experience with dragons, they can live a really long fucking time. I don't know ... but when we were fighting that bloke in Boston, I just got this sense he was old." I eyed Gethin. "Like Emerys' age."

"Not to sound like a total newbie here, but how do you know someone is a dragon?"

I didn't have an answer for that. Sure, I'd seen Taron, Talia, and a few others transform from human state to dragon form. But just seeing them walk by, I would have no way of knowing that they were hiding such immense power under the surface. Adding it to the list of questions I already had tallying up in my head for Taron's arrival.

Speaking of, it wouldn't do to have him wandering aimlessly about the castle. Nor was Avery's quarters an appropriate place to have our briefing session.

"I need to go make sure our guest gets to the right place. Gethin, meet us in the library when Avery's all set up."

"I'm good for now. I think I'm going to catch a nap if that's okay."

"After everything you've done for us the last week, you've earned it."

She gave me a grateful, if exhausted smile and plucked her glasses off, setting them on the bedside table before throwing herself atop the bed. I stepped back into the corridor and Gethin left the room, pulling the door shut behind him. I had my phone in hand, ready to send Taron an update on where to meet us when Gethin snatched the device from my fingers.

"Oi, what are you playing at?"

He studied the screen for a moment before he burst out laughing. "That's really what you're calling him?"

"You're just jealous I've got a dragon's number," I teased as I made a grab for the phone.

"You just had to go and flirt with a royal one," he quipped and tossed the device back to me.

"I'll have you know he flirted first," I snapped before sending off a message to Taron to meet in the library.

Belatedly, I realized two very important things: he had no bloody idea where the library was located and probably expected me to meet him to escort him officially. I let out a groan, not bothering to send a follow up message.

"Come on. We better go play chaperone," I said and started down to the main floor.

"You really think he is going to be able to tell us anything about who really took us out of commission?"

"He knew what the symbol meant when Avery cracked the system. And he looked properly freaked out about it, too."

"I guess I'm just struggling to see how dragons could be evil."

"Trust me, mate. I said the same thing, but I suppose any group has its good and bad. And we've just been lucky so far that we've only seen the good ones."

"Guess that's true." He went quiet as we rounded the last corner leading to the entry hall.

"What's going on in that head of yours?" I nudged his shoulder affectionately for good measure.

"It's going to sound foolish, but I felt a little left out when you all went off through the barrier without me."

"You really wanted to go?"

"Getting to see where you grew up, I don't know

... it helped me understand you in a way I hadn't expected."

"Well, not sure you'd have gotten much out of our trip to Boston. Though it was rather enlightening from a familial perspective."

He gave me a quizzical look. "I'm going to need more than that."

"So, the woman who showed up in the cave that sent me off to Boston. Apparently, she was a distant relative, a descendant of Emerys' cousin. She was a hero, and it was kind of like she was guiding us on our journey. I don't know ... it felt kind of nice to know there are places where I feel connected to my history even in the world I left behind."

"You having a relative who was a bona fide hero doesn't surprise me in the least. You're a Pendragon, Morgan. You've always had power in your blood. It had to come from somewhere. I suppose I never really considered that Emerys had left behind other relatives."

"I don't think she quite expected it either. It kind of messed her up for a bit."

"As much as I'd have loved to have gone with you, I'm kind of glad I didn't see that ..." He cleared his throat and adjusted his glasses yet again. "Sometimes you don't want to see your mentor struggle, you know?"

"Yeah, I get it."

We reached the entrance, and I picked up on the sound of voices just beyond the doorway. I marched forward and pushed the righthand door outward to find Taron arguing with one of the guards.

"You know who I am. I was here not a few hours ago with the Crown Princess."

"We are not prepared to receive you," the guard replied.

"I'll take him," I called, drawing their collective attention. "He's here at my invitation anyway."

"No one told us, Your Highness."

I bristled at the formality. "I wasn't aware I needed permission to invite a friend over."

The guard's jaw worked as he tried to formulate a response. I was fairly certain he was trying not to offend me, especially in front of a visiting royal.

"Why don't we go in? We have business to discuss," Taron said.

"Yes, let's go," I replied and motioned for him to enter.

The guard stepped aside and settled back into his post, jaw still working. I shut the door behind us, and Taron gave me a smile. "Your last message directed me to the library."

"Yeah, but I realized you probably had no idea where it was. Besides, if I'd left you to your own devices, you'd still be standing out there arguing."

"You have a point." He gestured for me to lead the way. "The library awaits."

I swallowed the lump in my throat and glanced at Gethin who'd remained silent during the whole exchange. "Come on, then. Off we go."

My friend let out an exasperated sigh as he looked from me to Taron and back again. "Don't let her fool you. She's got no clue where she's going either."

"Then it is an adventure we can take together," Taron replied with a laugh and looped his arm through mine.

My heart thudded erratically in my chest and the nape of my neck warmed at his touch. My mother's warning to tread carefully rang in my mind and the look of unease on Gethin's face signaled he worried about what this could mean, too. Taron appeared unconcerned by our closeness as we walked down the corridor.

"You looked nice during your mother's broadcast," Taron noted as Gethin moved ahead of us and took a turn down the corridor to our left.

"No, I didn't."

"Well, I suppose it is subjective. You always look nice to me."

"Do women really respond to lines like that? "

He smirked at me. "You can't deny you're a little bit flattered."

"Look, I think we can both agree there's something between us. You don't have to work so hard for it."

"Noted."

"Would you two hurry up?" Gethin called from around the corner.

We made the turn to find a set of inlaid wooden doors I'd not come across before—then again, I hadn't been here long enough to do a full exploration of the grounds—with Gethin standing by the handles. They appeared to be made of bronze. When he placed a hand on them, it gave an almost audible sigh; much like the door at Emerys' cabin had done on our first foray there after Nim's death. Had my mentor picked up that bit of magic from the castle? Or had she cast it long ago when she was queen?

"Don't tell me I'm missing some magical equivalent to a library card," I said as we crossed the threshold.

"You'll have to speak with the librarian about that," Gethin answered and made a beeline for a row of shelves that resembled a card catalog. He looked over his shoulder at Taron. "What was the name we're meant to be searching for?"

"The Syndicate of the First Inferno."

"Bit pretentious don't you think?" Gethin muttered.

"I would imagine most nefarious organizations have that in common," Taron answered and took stock of our surroundings.

The space felt both cozy and expansive. Shelves filled with meticulously kept volumes rose to the ceiling and rolling ladders sat at the end of each row ready to be used to retrieve items from the highest shelves. I scanned the rest of the space, expecting the aforementioned librarian to be seated at a desk somewhere, ready to silence us if we got too unruly. Though from what I could tell, we were alone.

"There should be a couple of texts in the ancient histories section," Gethin finally announced.

Wanting to make myself useful, I began scanning the shelves for anything that could give me a hint to where I might find the ancient histories section. While the rows were numbered, nothing obvious suggested what was contained within them. That was, until I ran a finger along what appeared to be a blank nameplate with my left hand. The bracelet around my wrist warmed and the metal shimmered, revealing etched text, letting me know I was in the literature section.

"You need to keep going," Gethin called, pointing several rows down. "Check the sixth shelf up, about midway down."

"Title would be helpful," I replied.

"*An Accounting of Albion's Uprisings*," he answered. "Specifically, volumes three and four."

That there were at least four volumes about the realm's uprisings unnerved me. It also made it painfully clear I was woefully uninformed about Camelot's history and that of its neighboring kingdoms. I made my way along the shelves, running my hand along each nameplate to reveal the subject matter until I found the Ancient Histories section.

I followed Gethin's instructions, climbing up to the sixth shelf and found the books, *An Accounting of Albion's Uprisings: Volume III* and *Volume IV*. They were thick leatherbound ledgers, each at least a thousand pages. I let out a groan as I did my best to carry the books down the ladder without dropping them. When I pivoted, I found Taron waiting to receive them. I gladly passed them along and together we wound our way to a table in a back corner. It had a quaint little lamp that reminded me of the tables at the Practitioner's Council. It made me miss Jules, but there wasn't any reason for her to be here. Not until we really understood what we were facing.

Gethin pulled one of the volumes towards him, and opened it to the index, scanning the small print at a rapid pace. Obviously, he listed speed reading among his talents alongside cooking. Good to know.

"Okay, let's see. Here it is," he said and flipped toward the middle of the book. "The Syndicate of the First Inferno began as a separatist movement nearly one thousand years ago, not long after the Dragon Court was formally recognized. They sought to keep dragon culture pure and refused to acknowledge the authority of the crown." He skimmed farther down the page and continued reading. "It is said that in its infancy, the Syndicate orchestrated several assassination attempts on the throne and royal family. But when those efforts failed, they turned their attention to instigating unrest among the kingdom's inhabitants and the surrounding realms."

"Sounds like a bunch of whiny fucks who were mad they weren't in charge," I muttered.

"They were much more than that," Taron said, his tone serious. "They came from the prior nobility and were skilled strategists and military leaders. They drew followers from every sector of our court life. They believed that dragon kind should not intermingle with fae or human life in any way."

"So, they wanted to be isolated from the rest of the world?"

"Precisely. And they abhorred any intermixing of bloodlines especially between the different races."

"Ugh, they're racists to boot."

"Yes. They fought for the purity of dragons."

"But why?"

"Because fae and human magic can be dangerous when mixed with our own."

He couldn't have mentioned that before?

"There was another reference in *Volume IV*," Gethin interjected.

Taron opened the book in front of him, flipping through to the start of the book. He passed it to me so I could read. I studied the small passage on the lefthand page.

"Although many believed the Syndicate had been stamped out nearly four hundred years ago, it is believed they were responsible for much of the recent violence and conflict among kingdoms. It is theorized that their disappearance and assumed eradication was in fact a purposeful campaign of misinformation on their part to conceal their true agenda in the modern age."

I looked at Taron. "They are still around."

"Most certainly, and they have adapted to the modern age. And I may know someone who can tell us what exactly they are planning."

THREE

Taron didn't give me a chance to ask who this mystery person was, with my next breath he was already on his feet and halfway to the exit. I scrambled after him, leaving Gethin to return the books.

"Wait a minute," I called, reaching out to grab Taron by the wrist.

He stopped and turned to face me. "Forgive me. I just thought that time was of the essence."

"You're going to need to give me more than you know someone who might be able to give us answers. Who is it? How do they know? And for that matter, how do you know so much about these arse-holes who apparently hate you and your ancestors?"

"All salient points." His jaw worked as if he intended to say more, but kept silent.

Oh, how I wished I could force it out of him.

"Well, we're not going anywhere until you answer at least one of them."

"Oh, don't worry about me, I'll just clean things up," Gethin called loudly, appearing behind the desk, and setting both thick volumes in the bin marked Returns.

I gave him an apologetic look before fixing Taron with a firm stare. "Go on."

"It really would be better if we discuss this once we are off the castle grounds."

"What, are you afraid someone might eaves-drop?" Gethin accused, gesturing toward himself.

"As I am sure you have noticed, these individuals are sophisticated. They have operated in the shadows for centuries, even after everyone thought them snuffed out. It would not surprise me if they had somehow installed spies within your ranks. After all, how do you suppose they so easily gained access?"

"Because they've got magic," I retorted.

"Fine, I will answer one question. I know so much because ancient orders are a fascination of mine. While everyone else was studying things like linguistics and tradecraft, I immersed myself in our realm's darker histories." He gave me an annoyed look. "Satisfied?"

"Not even remotely. But I get that's all you're going to share. So, let's go then. Where are we headed?"

"Shouldn't we inform someone we're leaving? Emerys, or the Queen maybe?" Gethin interjected.

Taron held up a hand. "The only 'we' involved are Morgan and me."

Gethin scoffed. "You don't really think anyone's going to let you take the Crown Princess anywhere without a chaperone?"

"They haven't seemed particularly bothered thus far."

My cheeks warmed as Gethin whirled to face me. "What?"

"It's not what you think ..." I let out a long exhale. "Gethin's right. Given everything that's happened, I would feel safer having him along. Which means the two of you need to stop trying to one up each other. You're both very manly and impressive."

"I wasn't ..." Gethin began, but averted his gaze.

"You're also right that we can't just go off without letting someone know. The last thing we need is everyone thinking I've been kidnapped again."

"I would not wish to cause you or your court any more strife. I will wait at the gate," Taron said and gave me a little bow before following the path we'd taken from the entry hall.

"You know he's just trying to impress you," Gethin muttered as we went in search of Emerys.

"He doesn't need to try," I noted.

"What did he mean you haven't needed a chaperone?"

"We are grown adults who are fully capable of looking after ourselves under normal circumstances."

"That doesn't answer the question, Morgan."

"We may have been meeting up by the cabin every now and then."

"Oh, well that explains a lot."

"Sod off," I said. "It's not like that. We've just talked and gotten to know each other."

"Right, and that's why he's listed as Hot Dragon Prince in your contacts."

"That's just stating fact," I quipped.

"Just be—"

"Careful. I know. I don't need another lecture from you too."

"I just don't want to see you get hurt."

"I appreciate your concern, but I'm a big girl. I can handle it."

He held up his hands in a placating gesture. "I'll drop it."

We reached Emerys' room and I knocked twice. Silence. I pushed the door inward, but found the room empty.

"Anywhere else she might go?" I glanced in Gethin's direction.

"She could be with the Queen."

We left the room and started for my mother's private chambers when I caught sight of Emerys at the far end of the corridor. She was in deep conversation with Shunae and another member of the diplomatic team. I could see the pin on his lapel.

Emerys spotted us, too, and gave the pair a nod before striding off, meeting Gethin and I halfway down the corridor. "You look as though you're on a mission." She gestured to my neck.

My hand went to the compass tucked beneath my shirt. It remained cool to the touch. "Not exactly. Well, we have a lead on these Syndicate bastards. But it's going to mean taking a little trip away from the castle."

"You don't appear to be seeking permission."

"Better to ask forgiveness," I answered. "We just wanted someone to know we were heading off."

"Do stay together," she advised.

"I won't leave her side. You have my word," Gethin said, his tone all seriousness and full of duty.

"I will inform your mother of your departure."

"Oh, and give Jules the head's up too when she gets back."

Emerys gave an assenting nod, and I felt a weight lift from my chest I hadn't been aware of until now. I had never needed anyone's blessing before—not even Nim's permission. Yet deep down, I knew I couldn't go traipsing off with Gethin and Taron without someone knowing since I could be missed.

"You don't have to actually stick by my side the whole time," I reminded Gethin as we reached the entryway.

"Given who we're traveling with, I'm not letting you two out of my sight."

"Prince Taron is waiting at the gate, Your Highness," announced the same guard from earlier when I stepped outside.

"Thank you."

I led the way past the stone where Excalibur had sat and for a moment, I could picture myself battered and bleeding as I freed the blade from its encasement. That day had changed everything, whether I was ready for it or not.

Taron stood at the gate, looking impatient. I wasn't used to him being in such a hurry. The gates opened and we left the palace grounds behind.

"So, do we get to know our destination now?" Gethin piped up.

"It is safer if you don't know the details. But we start by returning to my kingdom."

"That's a bit of a long trip."

"Our ultimate destination is actually not far from my workshop," he explained and tugged at the hem of his shirt.

"Not that I'm not eager for a show, but as you might recall, heights and I aren't exactly friends. So, the less time I have to spend airborne the better. I think I can get us close to your workshop."

He made a 'please proceed' gesture, and I raised my hands, tracing a circle in the air. I pictured the cliffside and the ocean, its salty spray hitting my face. The cave entrance sat ahead, and I could feel the warmth coming from within as his forges burned hot and ready to create his next treasure.

When I opened my eyes, the mouth of the cave sat neatly within the sphere I'd drawn. Even the air smelled different from the ambient atmosphere around us. I gestured for Taron to step through, and he moved through the space with an elegance that seemed decidedly him. A moment later, I ushered Gethin through before leaving Camelot behind and ending up in another kingdom entirely.

The ground beneath my feet was rocky and uneven, and I faltered. Both of my companions reached out to steady me. I was grateful for the support, but I couldn't help feeling like they were still competing with one another. Bloody male egos.

"So, where to from here?" Gethin asked, resituating his glasses.

"As I said, it is safer if you don't know the actual location."

"Then how are we supposed to get there?" Gethin demanded.

Taron gave me an apologetic look. "I am afraid that going airborne as you say cannot be avoided."

"If it's a short trip, I'll survive," I replied and turned to Gethin. "Well, I hope you aren't the type who gets all insecure in another man's presence."

Before Gethin could ask for clarification, Taron pulled off his shirt and shimmied out of his trousers. My friend's mouth went slack as the prince stood before us in all his naked glory. I couldn't help but smile.

"Just wait," I whispered.

"I—I just ... he's all ..."Gethin sputtered.

"You better get changed before he loses all ability to speak," I called to Taron.

"Of course. I wouldn't want to render your friend mute."

Gethin glared at me, but turned his back. I'd seen Taron make the transition from human to dragon enough times now that it no longer caught me off guard.

"Uh, wait, before you do, you ought to make sure you've got something to change into when we get wherever it is we're going." Despite his affinity for going au naturale I wasn't sure other dragons felt the same. And Taron may no longer be next in line to the throne, but he was still royalty and that mattered.

"A good point," Taron said and I watched him dart into the cave, returning a moment later with a leather bag. He scooped up his discarded clothing and tossed it inside before holding it out to me. "If you would be so kind?"

I took the strap and slung it over my shoulder. I made a shooing motion, and he took a step back before his body grew vibrant and tinged orange. Scales rippled over his flesh and in moments, a massive creature sat where the man had stood.

"Right up you get," I told Gethin as Taron opened one of his front claws.

"Excuse me?"

"You didn't think we were going to ride him. That's just rude, " I quipped and settled in the other outstretched claws.

"As you're so fond of saying, this is mental," Gethin complained as he arranged himself.

With a single flap of his enormous wings, Taron took to the sky. I'd half wondered if he intended to blindfold us. As it turned out, it wasn't necessary. He reached such heights that I felt ice form on my eyelashes, crusting over my eyes so I could hardly see. Somehow, I could just make out the sound of Gethin's teeth chattering above the gusts of wind trying to knock us off course.

After what had felt like an hour, Taron descended back toward the ground. The air around us warmed. He let out a few puffs of cloudy breath, his chest warming enough to abate the chill that had settled in my bones. My lashes unstuck and I could see again.

He set us down in a field that had seen better

days. I could make out where rows of plants had once sat, offering a harvest of some kind. But the soil sat barren and forgotten now. The hard-packed ground smelled oddly of sulfur. My gut told me nothing could grow here.

A short distance away, Gethin bent double, trying to catch his breath. When he straightened, I could just make out the annoyance on his face. He wiped the fog from his glasses. "You do that on a regular basis?"

"No. Believe me, I prefer portal travel."

Behind us, Taron shifted back to human form, running his hands through his dark curls to free them of tiny shards of ice. Apparently even he wasn't immune from the elements in the atmosphere. He held out his hand for the bag and I tossed it to him. Once he'd dressed, he passed the bag to me again.

"I know you have many questions. If the person we are here to see agrees to help, then I swear you will get answers. But he is a bit of a recluse and distrustful of strangers. It took me a very long time to gain his trust. So please, I beg you to stay silent."

I mimed zipping my lips. "Won't say a word."

"You as well." He eyed Gethin warily.

"You have my word, I won't say anything."

"This way."

He led us from the field through a small stand of trees and next to the side of a mountain range. Tiny outcroppings of rock dotted the sides of the mountains. I could see smoke coming from one high up. Bloody hell, with our luck that was our destination. I really hated heights.

"It's not far now," Taron called and started along a dusty path. I could make out faint footprints as we walked. Someone had definitely traveled this way before.

"How much can we really trust him?" Gethin whispered in my ear.

"Oh, come on, enough. He hasn't done a single thing to make me question if he's an ally."

"Don't you find it strange he just happens to have a connection who knows about the shadow organization who attacked us?"

"He's allowed to have hobbies." I let out a huff. "You just don't like that I fancy someone."

"We've been through this. I like you Morgan, but not in that way. I just don't want to see you get hurt or find yourself in a situation that puts your kingdom or future at risk."

"I highly doubt one romantic fling would upend my future."

"You never know."

"If you two are done whispering about me behind my back, we've arrived," Taron called from around the next bend of the mountain path.

I picked up the pace and rounded the mountain to find a large hole directly ahead of us. I glanced at Taron. "How are we going to do this?"

"Just stay behind me."

I fell into step beside Gethin, and we remained half a pace behind Taron as he walked into the cave. The space was carved out, like someone had purposely cleared it away. It was tall enough for all three of us to stand up comfortably and the air wasn't as stuffy as I'd expected. After perhaps two or three feet, the trajectory of the cave shifted, angling downward. Tiny lights dotted either side of the stone walls as we continued inward. They weren't like anything I'd seen before and when I got closer, I could just make out what looked like tiny glowing figures, and it sent nervous shivers down my spine.

The cave finally opened up into a large space, not unlike Taron's workshop and I briefly wondered if this recluse had come out of hiding just to help the prince construct his comfort zone. The lighting within the chamber was more than what I'd expect —electric bulbs spaced out, connected with a single running wire down to a switch on the far wall. Computers and monitors were inlaid into the stone on the far wall and a surprisingly modern chair sat in front of the tech. The chair spun and its occupant stood up.

"Prince Taron. To what do I owe this unexpected visit?"

"Vilmar, I've come to speak with you about the Syndicate. I'm afraid they aren't as vanquished as we once thought."

FOUR

Vilmar considered Taron's words in silence. His piercing gaze slid across our group, settling on me. I did my best not to squirm as the silence persisted. Finally, he looked at Gethin with that same intensity. Taron looked unconcerned by the other man's inspection.

"The quest for knowledge has always been ours alone," Vilmar said in a deep voice. "Yet, you bring outsiders?"

"I know you value your privacy, old friend," Taron said, taking a step forward. "But they need to know what you can tell us. They need your perspective."

"You get the news up here?" I blurted before I could stop myself.

Vilmar and Taron both glared at me. "My kingdom nearly ended up in ruins because of some ancient pricks and Taron says you know all about them. I need to find them, so you're going to tell me everything you know."

Taron closed the distance between us and when he spoke his voice came out in a sharp whisper. "You gave me your word you would remain silent."

"But we don't have time for niceties."

"I warned you Vilmar was a recluse and distrustful of others," he reminded me.

"Ah, you must be the wayward princess," Vilmar declared, his tone held no bite.

"Forgive her disrespect. She was raised without proper manners."

I bristled at Taron's dig. "My aunt raised me just fine, thank you."

"I mean you no disrespect, Vilmar in bringing them here. I am only trying to keep peace amongst the realm."

Vilmar rubbed his chin and considered Taron's words. Beside me, Gethin stood still as a statue. If it weren't for the slight bob of his Adam's apple signaling he was still breathing, I'd be worried my friend had been scared to death.

In one fluid motion much like I'd seen Taron do,

Vilmar rose, his body undulating almost snakelike as he approached. It was then that I caught the milky cataract in one of his eyes. How I'd missed it from his prior examination of me, I couldn't say.

"You are not like the royals I have encountered before."

"Yeah, I get that a lot."

How many have you encountered huddled up here in your cave?

I nodded toward the tech set up. "That got access to the internet?"

Vilmar smiled and I could see sharp teeth pressed against his lips. "I can access a great many things, your highness."

That filled me with less confidence than he'd probably intended. I looked back to Taron. "What is it you think he knows that can help us?"

Taron blew out his breath and for the first time, I saw worry lines wrinkling the otherwise flawless skin around his eyes and lips. "When I wanted to study the Syndicate, to prepare myself to combat them if they should rise again, I found Vilmar shared a similar interest. He has the single largest collection of Syndicate artifacts in the kingdom."

"I can see you are not impressed with words," Vilmar said. "Come, let me show you."

He spun on his heel and marched off toward a doorway carved into the rockface opposite to where we'd entered. Gethin regained control of his limbs and looped one arm through mine. The way his body trembled told me he was truly unsettled by our host.

"Awfully convenient he's got the largest collection," he whispered in my ear.

"I was thinking the same thing," I replied.

I didn't want to believe Taron would lead us astray. He seemed so genuine in his interest in learning and gaining knowledge. And the connection we shared felt like so much more than just physical. It was a magnetic pull I couldn't fight. I refused to believe the universe would put him in my path if he meant me ill.

"This way. Come along," Vilmar called up ahead.

I picked up the pace, dragging Gethin with me as we emerged into another chamber, this one lit by softer lights hanging from a web of wires overhead. They cast warm glowing pools of light over several old manuscripts and partially intact scrolls.

"Given their age, I ask that you not touch them without proper protection," Vilmar called.

A box of linen gloves materialized on the table in front of me. I plucked two from the box and pulled them on before bending over the first scrap of paper.

"How old is this?" The ink was nearly faded, but I could pick out the symbol I'd seen at the office in Boston and on the computer system Avery had dismantled.

"It dates back nearly eight hundred years." Vilmar sounded proud of his antiquities.

I looked up at the man standing at the far end of the table. "Tell me something about them I couldn't read in a book or from one of these scrolls."

"Well, they believed in the purity of blood. not just for dragon kind, mind you. They recognized that the fae and mortals had a place in this world, but they thought it safer if everyone kept to themselves."

"Something about the magic mixing being too volatile," I said.

"More in line with maintaining order."

"You mean oppressing other beings," Gethin muttered.

"They bore the mark you see on that parchment as a way to identify one another," Vilmar continued. "A simple brand would have been insufficient given the nature of a shifted dragon's scales."

"There are a couple of written accounts of the

process. I never made it all the way through," Taron volunteered. "They were brutal and barbaric."

"Magic bound them together. Magic and dragon fire." The way Vilmar's milky eye lit up at the words set me on edge.

"So, what, once you're in you can never get out again?"

"Why would you want to?" he continued. "At least, that is what the early adopters believed."

The way he spoke suggested this came from more than just reading written accounts. "I know it's not polite to ask a woman her age and I suppose it applies to dragons, too, but you understand why I need to ask."

He gestured at me and gave Taron an amused look. "You best be careful with this one."

"You're stalling," I said.

"I am much older than the establishment of the kingdom in which we stand."

I'd been afraid of that. Gethin took another step toward me and his right hand pressed tight on my left wrist. I didn't need to look at him to understand what he was suggesting. The thought had crossed my mind, too. We were in unfamiliar territory and if things went sideways, I'd need to defend myself. I could almost feel Excalibur buzzing with potential energy, ready to defend me and my allies.

"And let me guess, you came by these documents firsthand?"

"Oh, you are far cleverer than many give you credit for," Vilmar said, a smile playing at his lips.

Taron's face clouded with confusion. "You told me you purchased them from other collectors."

Vilmar smiled and this time the points of his teeth signaled the menace lying beneath the mask of calm. "You believed what I wanted you to believe. You were always so trusting. I was not at all surprised when you chose to abdicate your claim. You were not meant to rule."

I reached out my hand and pulled Taron back to stand shoulder to shoulder with me. "Where would they usually brand their members?" I addressed Taron.

"Originally, on their backs. But I've heard that changed about six hundred years ago. Something about camouflaging it."

Something told me Vilmar was definitely old school. He might have a lair full of tech, but he was bloody ancient, and I doubted he'd want to change the mark branding him one of these purist nutters. I bet he got some perverse pleasure out of it.

"Now might be a good time to leave," Gethin said.

Vilmar let out another laugh. "You don't really think you're walking out of here, boy."

"Oi, you don't get to talk to my friends like that you condescending fuck," I snapped.

Without thinking, I pressed my right index finger to the tiny sapphire on the bracelet around my left wrist. I stepped back as the metal twisted and elongated.

"Foolish girl. You think a dragon-forged blade frightens me?"

"No, but my sword thinks you're as big a dick as I do, and it's got something to say about it."

"Morgan, stop antagonizing the scary dragon," Gethin hissed.

"I have to agree with him," Taron replied.

"Yes, princess, listen to your betters," Vilmar mocked, and his eyes took on a hint of orange.

He leaned back and a fireball erupted from his mouth, hurtling straight for Gethin's chest. I shoved him out of the way and brought the flat of Excalibur's blade up to block the attack. Sweat broke out along my brow and along the small of my back as the flames licked at me. Finally, the assault ended, and I let out a gasp.

Out of the corner of my eye, I spotted Taron round the far side of the chamber. His hands hung loose at his sides, and it appeared Vilmar didn't see him coming. Well, that was until Taron's left foot hit a bit of loose rock on the floor. Vilmar's head whipped around, and his hands shifted into talons.

For a split second I was back in the office in Boston facing the man who'd orchestrated Avery's attack. His hands had transformed in the same manner. I'd been so focused on assuming he was fae I didn't even consider it was a partial shift to his dragon form.

"Look out!" I shouted just as Taron narrowly missed the scrape of a sizzling claw. The momentum of his dodging carried him forward and he was able to snag the hem of the other man's shirt, yanking it back over his shoulders.

On Vilmar's back, situated neatly between his shoulder blades sat the Syndicate's mark. It shimmered with an orange glow as he moved. It looked far more like a tattoo than a brand. He let out a howl as he tried to buck off Taron's grip.

"Grab everything you can," Taron called. "I can't hold him much longer."

I tossed the bag to Gethin and approached the pair of dragons, sword still in hand. I held Excalibur's tip below Vilmar's throat. "Was it you who took Camelot offline?"

"Oh, your highness. That is for me to know and you to wonder," he taunted and laughed.

Excalibur practically vibrated in my hand, inching ever closer to slicing the man's arteries. But I wasn't a killer. I pulled my hand back and willed the sword into its inert state. It shifted again into the jewelry Taron had fashioned for me. Careful not to let Vilmar's hands touch me, I raised a fist and slammed it hard into his jaw. I felt a bone crack and wasn't entirely convinced I hadn't just shattered my hand.

The force was enough to crack the back of his head against Taron's shoulder and he crumpled to the ground. Taron staggered to catch his balance just as a fine red mist filled the periphery of my vision. Shit.

"We need to get out of here now. That shit's toxic."

"Are we going to have to worry about any more of them?" Gethin asked, already beginning to cough.

"Worry about that later. We need to get out of here first," I replied and offered Taron a hand.

He took it and held it in a vicelike grip. With my other hand, I grabbed Gethin by the elbow and started for the entrance we'd come through. The mist thickened at floor level, and I could feel an uncomfortable itching sensation against my legs. I broke out into a sprint, dragging both men along behind me until we were in the antechamber with the tech again. The mist was less intense here and I hurried to the winding path that would take us out of the cave system and back to clean air.

The freshness of the atmosphere had never smelled so sweet as we emerged minutes later. Gethin bent double, gasping for breath. I gave him a few solid slaps on the back to try and help clear his lungs.

"He needs to be seen by a physician," Taron said. "I can get us there."

"No offense ... but I don't ... trust you," Gethin gasped before falling into a hacking fit.

"Vilmar fooled everyone," I said. "And he's not wrong. You need medical attention, Gethin."

"Showing up at the palace would raise questions here," Taron said. "Give me two minutes."

"You've got ninety seconds," I replied as I tried to help Gethin into a more comfortable position.

"Bet you wish you'd stayed home this time?" I said.

"What and miss you ... in action?"

"Save your breath, mate," I prompted.

When Taron came back into view, I spotted a cell phone in hand. "It isn't ideal, but we need to get back to my workshop. Help will meet us there."

"He's not in any condition to be in the air again," I said.

"Can you portal us there?"

The adrenaline was beginning to wear off from having socked a centuries-old dragon in the jaw and my stomach rumbled, reminding me it had been far too long since I'd eaten anything. "Uh, yeah. I can get us there."

"Then we need to go."

I stood and focused on a spot a brief distance ahead of me. I pictured the cave again, felt the sea air pepper my cheeks and envisioned it helping Gethin ease his breathing. I traced a circle midair and when I opened my eyes, the cave once more sat ahead of us. Without a word, Taron bent and hoisted Gethin to his feet, careful to support my friend as they walked through. I spared a glance at the mountain behind me and couldn't help but feel as though eyes were watching me. Vilmar would need to be dealt with, but getting Gethin help took priority. Yet Gethin's point about others being out there rang in my head. If they'd managed to remain hidden for centuries and branded themselves with magic, I didn't doubt they had a way to communicate that was untraceable to outsiders.

"You're not going to get away with this," I proclaimed to the empty space around me.

Through the portal I could see Gethin and Taron disappear into the mouth of his workshop. My temple ached as the spell fazed in and out at the edges. I was running out of time. I stepped through the portal, and everything tilted off its axis. Maybe the mist had taken a toll on me, and I hadn't realized it in the moment. Or maybe my penchant for forgetting to eat was catching up to me, but everything swayed, and my head went fuzzy.

"Morgan?" Taron's concerned voice came from miles off and I could barely see the outline of his body before my vision tunneled to darkness.

FIVE

Smell came back to me first—ash and metal in the air. Somehow my brain knew it wasn't a dangerous place. At least not on purpose. I also caught the musk of a familiar body and I tried to settle back into the darkness. I was safe.

Sound flooded me next, bringing with it hacking coughs from nearby. It only took a split second for my mind to register the sound as Gethin. He was still hurt. That was enough to rouse me. I opened my eyes to find myself lying on the small cot in the corner of Taron's workshop. Gethin lay on the floor on his side, his body shaking with each convulsive expulsion of mist. I could see it filtering up through the large gap in the ceiling.

I tried to stand, but my vision went fuzzy at the

edges. I sank back into a sitting position. Taron appeared in my line of sight. He wore only a pair of stained pants—likely something he kept here if he decided to fly in. Even he wasn't reckless enough to try welding in the nude.

"You better tell me what the hell happened," Talia's voice demanded.

The Crown Princess appeared in view next, looking cross with her brother. But the moment her gaze fell on Gethin, it softened to one of concern.

"Heal now, berate later," Taron answered, ushering her toward Gethin.

"Is he going to be okay?" I called, my voice hoarse.

"Talia is an excellent healer. Your friend is in good hands," Taron answered, closing the distance between us, he placed a hand on my cheek. "You, Morgan, had me worried."

"I didn't inhale nearly as much of that crap."

"But you collapsed as soon as your portal closed."

I waved off his concern. "I just need to eat something. If Gethin wasn't over there coughing up a lung, he'd be chiding me about it."

"I am sorry I put you both in danger."

"Like I said, he fooled you, too. He's old as dirt

and manipulative. He had centuries to build the facade he knew you'd gravitate toward. I bet he cozied up to you, because you were the heir. What better way to influence current events than to have the ear of the next king?"

"Who manipulated my brother?" Talia looked over Gethin's shoulder at me as she rubbed something into his chest.

"I told you, focus on your patient," Taron said.

Talia shrugged. "I can multitask."

"Vilmar," I answered for him.

Talia visibly shuddered. "Oh, he's creepy."

"You just didn't like him, because he lived in a cave," Taron muttered.

"Some stereotypes exist for a reason," she countered. "But how was he influencing you?"

"Turns out he's one of the original founding members of the Syndicate of the First Inferno," I explained, feeling my energy increase as I talked.

"He did this?"

"Filled the room with this nasty mist. I thought we'd gotten out before it got too bad, but Gethin bore the brunt of it."

"I can see that. This salve should ease his breathing," she explained as I pushed myself to my feet.

Taron trailed close behind me as I moved to

kneel at Gethin's side. He wasn't coughing nearly as much, and his pallor looked much improved. But he also looked worn out.

"Why don't you have a lie down over there and rest a bit?" I urged him.

"We need to ... warn them," Gethin mumbled.

"It will keep. You need rest."

With Talia's help, I hoisted Gethin to his feet and we laid him on the bed. He gave a small cough and more mist dribbled from his lips.

"That stuff is likely doing nasty things to his insides the longer it's in his lungs."

"Hmm ... There is one other thing I could try, but it is dangerous."

"You are not putting your life at risk," Taron interjected.

"Well, you aren't trained for it, so you don't get a say," she retorted.

"What is it?"

"I can draw it out from him all at once."

"That doesn't sound so bad."

"It's incredibly painful for your friend. And if I'm not fast enough to burn it away with fire, well we could all basically die."

Well, fuck.

"Right, let's hope you're fast enough."

"He needs to rest and rebuild his strength. And you look like you could use a meal."

"I don't want to leave him."

"I'll be back."

Without another word, Talia left the workshop and I hovered beside Gethin as Taron stood a short distance away. He looked at me with such intensity I feared his gaze could ignite flames all on their own.

"You're mad at me. Go on and just say it," I prompted.

"I am not accustomed to people giving their word and then so quickly breaking it."

"I know I should have kept my mouth shut. I'm sorry, but I just got a bad vibe off the guy."

He stepped toward me and cupped my cheek again. "But ... had you not spoken up, we might all be dead now."

"Is that your way of saying thank you?"

"In part."

He leaned in closer until I could feel his breath against my skin. It was warm, just like his touch. The way he studied me with his eyes drinking in every curve and angle of my jawline made me not want to lose the contact.

"Can you ... get a room?" Gethin coughed from beside us.

The moment broke and I stepped back, laughing. Taron looked momentarily annoyed that Gethin had interfered with his ability to kiss me, but the tension vanished.

"You should rest, too, while we wait for Talia's return," Taron urged.

"What are you going to do?"

He pointed to the bag of pilfered artifacts from Vilmar's collection. "I haven't had much chance to study these particular artifacts. I see now he kept them at a distance to keep me curious, but not give me enough information to see through his deception."

My stomach growled, reminding me that food was in fact essential for getting anything else done. But there wasn't much else I could do about that predicament until Talia came back. So, I sat on the floor and settled against the edge of the cot, my head resting in line with Gethin's ribcage. I watched as Taron cleared space on a worktable and gently laid the bag's contents out. His hands shifted, the skin replaced with scales, just enough to avoid secreting oils onto the aged parchment.

"How long did you know Vilmar?" I asked, eyes closing halfway as the ambience of the cave lulled me toward sleep.

"Since I began studying the Syndicate ..." Taron replied, stopping what he was doing, staring off into the distance. "From the time I was about twelve or thirteen."

"And no one thought it was weird the king's son was running off chatting up an ancient dragon in a cave somewhere?"

"I have always enjoyed a certain freedom, even before I stepped aside in favor of Talia. They were simply happy I had found something that engaged my mind."

"You didn't tell them what you were actually studying, did you?"

Taron's dark complexion warmed, and he ducked his head. "Not at first. And when they did finally press me on the topic I'd found so fascinating, Vilmar had given me ways to explain how it was for the protection of our kingdom. Understanding one's enemy as deeply as possible."

"He coached you," I pointed out. "He was using you. I mean, if the Syndicate had vanished from society hundreds of years ago, why even teach you about them now?"

Taron set a leatherbound journal down and turned to look at me. I could tell by the way his shoulders and pectorals tensed he was holding back his emotions. "I realize now that I was misled."

I pushed myself to my feet, closing the distance between us. "And doesn't that make you pissed off?"

His voice dropped in pitch. "I am furious."

"Because that wanker lied to you."

"Yes."

"Then be angry."

"It is not appropriate to—" he began, but I cut him off.

"Look, I don't know where this quest is going to take us next, but you're going to need a clear head. We all are. So, get angry, throw shit, punch a wall. Do whatever it is dragons do to get shit off their chests."

His jaw worked and his eyes sparkled with pent-up emotion. "Believe me, I wish to do a great many things ... but I don't want you to think less of me."

"I think maybe we could both use a reminder that you're still human," I said, reaching up I pressed my palm to his cheek. "I'll stay with Gethin. You go do what you have to do."

"You are too good to me."

"We all get a little messy sometimes."

He closed his eyes to stave off tears as he tugged his shirt over his head and laid it over the edge of a stool before disappearing from view. I felt the air pressure shift as his mass changed and heard a guttural roar from just beyond the cave entrance. I couldn't help myself, so I ducked into the entryway and watched Taron in his dragon form as he thrashed around on the cliff edge before taking to the sky. Bright yellow-white bursts of flame erupted from his mouth in what I could only call screams.

My chest ached as I watched him disappear into the clouds. I couldn't blame him for being furious at the betrayal. And as I retreated inside the cave I couldn't shake the thought that I'd just made it worse by pushing him to confront those feelings. Had I rubbed it in his face that he'd been played?

The sound of Gethin's coughing pulled me from my woe-is-me spiral. He sat up, clutching at his ribs as he gasped for air. I looked around, hoping to find more of the salve Talia had used to ease his breathing. Wasn't it meant to last longer than this, or had she been gone for more time than I'd realized given Taron's emotional breakdown?

"Easy, mate," I said, moving to sit beside Gethin.

"It hurts," he rasped.

"I know. I'm so sorry I got you into this."

I pressed my right hand to the middle of his back and rubbed in gentle circles, pouring a little bit of magic into the gesture to ease his discomfort. He coughed a few more times, but it didn't sound nearly as labored or violent. Except when I pulled my hand away, my fingers ached, and I could almost see tiny blisters popping out along the length of my hand. Apparently using magic to try and ease his pain was only going to make us both suffer.

"We're going to get you fixed up," I assured, trying not to let the ache in my hand preoccupy me.

"Guess this ... is what ... I get ... for wanting ... to be ... part of the ... team," he choked out.

"Come on, save your breath," I urged and pressed him back toward the pillow and the mattress.

Footsteps sounded on the rocks outside the cave, and I straightened in time to find Talia reappear carrying a bag slung over one shoulder. Her dark curls reminded me so much of Taron, flying out behind her in a wave as she came to a stop.

"Where's Taron?"

"Working through some things," I answered, gesturing to Gethin. "He's getting worse."

She grabbed my wrist and studied the red splotches on my hand. "You tried to help, didn't you?"

"Like I said, he got worse, and you were gone ... I didn't know what else to do."

She let out an exasperated sigh. "I've got something that should ease the pain for that, but you're right, helping your friend is priority."

"What can I do to help?"

I half-expected her to snap at me to stay out of her way. Instead, Talia rummaged in her bag and handed over a parcel wrapped in butcher paper. I picked up the scent of spiced meats and my mouth watered. "Eat something. It doesn't do us any good if you pass out from hunger."

I unwrapped the food and stepped back to the stool where Taron had left his shirt, setting it in my lap as I sat down. I was only mildly concerned he hadn't returned yet. For all that I claimed to know about the prince, I didn't have the faintest idea how he handled his emotions. All I'd seen up until now was the suave, sexy man who enjoyed a good flirt.

I took a bite of the sandwich and studied Talia as she worked. She moved quickly, but quietly around the cot, laying out little stumpy candles around Gethin's body. "You need to lay as still as you can," she instructed him.

After taking a few more bites, I set the food aside, remembering her warning that whatever she was about to do to my friend was going to be painful. I could already feel my stomach twisting itself into knots. I almost wished Taron would hurry and come back, so I could lean on him for support. As if on cue, Taron stood at the mouth of the cave with sunlight dappling his bare skin. He looked a bit worn out, but in better spirits.

"What have I missed?" he asked, retrieving his shirt.

"She's just starting," I replied.

"I'm going to need you two to be quiet so I can focus," Talia ordered.

Without asking, Taron slid his hand into mine and gave it a squeeze. "She knows what she's doing," he assured me.

My grip on his hand tightened as Talia blew out a tiny flame from her lips. It settled on the tip of her right index finger, and she bent down, using it to light each of the tiny candles around him. Gethin coughed a few more times as he tried to lay still, the light reflecting on the lenses of his glasses in such a way that I couldn't make out his pupils.

More puffs of red mist filled the air as Gethin hacked before settling against the pillow. My right hand ached in time with the mist as it dispersed. Whoever came up with that shit was a vile and vindictive bastard, and if they weren't already long-dead, they deserved to be shot.

Once all of the candles were lit, Talia stepped back. She held her hands out over Gethin's body, as if tracing the contours of his torso. Her dark skin shifted to bronze scales up to the elbow and her fingernails sharpened into claws, much like Vilmar had done and the man I'd fought in Boston. I barely repressed a shiver as she flexed her changed fore-arms. I bit my tongue to keep from interrupting with questions about what exactly she intended to do to save my friend's life. Gethin's hands trembled as he gripped the thin blanket beneath him.

"I'm sorry," Talia whispered before I felt a rush of air as power rippled through the space, and Gethin screamed.

CHAPTER

SIX

I reacted on instinct. My body lunged towards Gethin's painful wails and only Taron's firm embrace kept me from interfering with the magic Talia worked. The few bites of sandwich I'd eaten rolled in my gut, threatening to make a repeat appearance as Gethin writhed on the cot, his skin turning ashen.

"I know it hurts, but you need to stay still," Talia prompted.

I didn't think Gethin heard her since his body thrashed from side to side. His pallor flashed to a deep red outlining all of his veins and arteries, forcing them to bulge unnaturally beneath his skin. When his head turned toward me, I could make out tear tracts on his cheeks.

"You have to stop," I shouted.

"I can't," Talia replied, not looking at me.

Her shifted fingers spread out and she pushed them downward over Gethin's chest. His body went still. I strained to hear the rasp of his breathing, but the workshop was eerily silent. My pulse thrummed in my neck, making black spots pop in my vision as I waited for something, anything, to happen. The dark veins along Gethin's arms and face looked ready to burst and I had to turn away, burying my head in Taron's shoulder. He shifted his weight to place himself in front of me, further obscuring my view.

Sound ebbed and flowed as my brain tried to both register what was happening around me and block out the horror my friend was enduring. I picked out the scuffing of Talia's shoes against the cave floor as she moved around the cot. I heard the mattress groan as weight pressed against it. Was she sitting beside him, trying to ease his suffering? Or was she about to plunge her talons into his chest?

"Prepare yourself, brother," Talia warned.

Her voice sounded oddly rough and distorted, like she was speaking through too many teeth. I lifted my head and peered over Taron's shoulder long enough to see that her facial features had transformed into the snout of a dragon. Dark bronze scales tapered to the tip of her nose, and I watched transfixed as she lifted her hands up.

Taron's back tensed as his own body changed. I could hear him give a soft grunt as thick wing joints erupted from his back, spreading outward, spanning the available space in the cave. They shimmered in the candlelight, matching Talia's metallic features. With a deft movement, Taron's wings folded around us both, blocking my view.

But I need to see.

I struggled against his embrace, trying to twist my body, so I had some idea what was about to happen. Except Taron held firm, his legs planted like ancient tree trunks in the ground. He wasn't going anywhere, no matter how much I wanted him to move.

"It's almost over," he whispered.

All at once, Gethin let out another ear-splitting shriek and I could taste bile on the back of my tongue. Around us the air began to cloud with red mist. I tensed, trying not to inhale. Talia had said if she wasn't able to burn it away, we'd all die. As if activated by the mist's presence, my right hand burned, the tiny blisters growing angrier and threatening to burst. My heart hammered and my body swayed.

Crackling flames erupted from just over Taron's shoulder. The mist vanished, bit by bit as Talia turned, blowing her dragon's breath around. As I'd guessed, I broke out in a sweat due to the closeness of the fire. But at least it meant I wasn't dead. The flames died down and my ears strained for any sounds that Gethin remained with us. The silence that followed was agonizing. Taron still wouldn't let me go, his wings wrapped protectively around us.

"Gethin," I finally called.

A moan came in response. "Ow."

Relief flooded me, washing away my own discomfort and pain from the blisters. Somehow, I pushed away from Taron, managing to duck beneath one of his massive wings and fell to my knees beside the cot. "You're alive."

"Is that what you call this?" he asked and for the first time since the incident not breaking out in a coughing fit every two words.

I looked up at Talia, who had already reverted to human form as she snuffed out the candles that were now barely nubs. "I don't know how you knew how to do that, but thank you for saving his life."

"My brother has his curiosities and so do I. From

the time I was ten, I studied medicine. I figured I ought to have a skill to fall back on if the whole being queen thing doesn't work out." Her smirk betrayed a hint of amusement in her tone.

"I owe you," I said, standing and offering my hand more from habit.

She turned it over in her own, studying the red bumps on my skin and frowned. "I honestly expected this to go away with the rest of it."

"Would some of the salve you gave Gethin earlier help?" I suggested.

She shook her head. "No. That medicine is meant specifically to ease breathing. This is more of a contact wound from the magic working through his system."

"Did you get all of it?" Taron questioned.

Talia shot her brother an annoyed look. "Yes, I know what I'm doing."

"Then, uh, how do I get rid of this?" I tried to flex my fingers and winced in pain.

Talia turned my hand over in hers again. "I mean, it would be horribly uncomfortable, but we could try to burst them and relieve the pressure."

"Yeah, no ... let's not do that." My stomach lurched at the mental image it conjured.

"Excalibur," Gethin exclaimed from his position on the cot.

"What?" Talia and I turned to look at him in unison.

"It's protected you before. Maybe it can heal you? It was forged with dragon magic after all."

Well, it wasn't something I'd have considered before, but he wasn't wrong. Excalibur and I were linked by blood magic that allowed the blade to recognize me as a Pendragon, and it was forged by dragons. Maybe it really could purge the dark magic from my flesh. Of course, that assumed I could get the sword to transform without it reacting defensively to the wounds.

"Uh, I might need some help." I held up my left wrist for Talia and waved my hand to make the bracelet jangle. "Mind taking it off?"

She cast Taron a nervous look as she undid the clasp. She laid the bracelet out across her left palm and offered it to me. Thinking through the transformation, I was fairly certain she wouldn't want to be holding it.

"Maybe just set it down," I said, and gestured to one of Taron's empty work benches.

She placed it on the hard surface and moved

away. I gingerly pressed my aching right index finger to the sapphire at the end. To my relief, the bracelet shimmered, taking on the shape of the sword without hesitation. The blade somehow gleamed bright white even without a light source as I stood next to it.

Please let this work.

My hand shook as I held it over the blade. Like a magnet drawing its opposing pole in close, the blade shimmered, and my hand slammed down against the flat of it. The very edge nicked my palm, and I winced as blood dribbled onto the work bench. I felt bad for ruining Taron's space, but it turned out I didn't need to worry. The sword absorbed the blood and the spots where my fingers had made contact with the metal turned an angry shade of reddish purple. The color almost resembled how Gethin's veins had looked as Talia worked her healing magic. I gritted my teeth as my hand ached. I wanted to pull it away, but the sword continued to drink up the blood.

One by one, the blisters receded, leaving behind pink flesh that smoothed out and regained normal coloring. Finally, the sword's glowing failed and my hand stopped bleeding. The magnetic pull that had kept me immobile vanished and I lifted my hand, examining it.

"Well shit, that actually worked. Good one, Gethin!"

"Yes, well done," Talia said, giving him an approving nod.

"Not that I'm not happy that worked, but shouldn't we warn the Queen and the Council about Vilmar and his connection to the Syndicate?"

"You don't think he'd be foolish enough to try something else right now, do you?"

"If he is connected to them like you say, he won't be working alone," Talia noted.

"There is no if. I saw his mark myself. For all I know, he is one of the founding members," Taron said. "But you are correct, he is most certainly not working alone. He may be manipulative, but I have spent enough time with him to know he prefers things done in the old ways."

"But he had all that tech," I pointed out.

"Yes. Someone else had to have put it there, I have no doubt."

I looked at Gethin. His cheeks were flushed, and his chest rose and fell with shallow breaths. He was in no condition to travel back to Camelot by air. I picked up the sandwich I'd discarded and shoved the rest of it in my mouth. I was going to need all the energy I could to get us home.

THE SEA AIR outside of Taron's workshop smacked me in the face as I stood on the rocks. Gethin was finally on his feet of his own accord. Taron and Talia stood off to one side, speaking in low whispers.

"What do you think the Queen will do when we tell her what happened?" Gethin asked, leaning on my shoulder for support.

"Honestly, no idea. But if she's smart, she'll hunt Vilmar down and get him to confess to what he did. Maybe even give up his accomplices."

"Something tells me if he's stayed off of everyone's radar this long, he won't be easy to hunt down, or break."

"Yeah, I suppose that's true." I had half a mind to try and track the bastard down myself.

"You two should get going," Taron called, stepping away from his sister.

I gestured for him to join me. "You ought to come along, too. I'm sure my mother will want a full picture of what we found."

"No, I should return and notify my own court," Taron protested.

"I will make sure our parents are aware of what you've uncovered," Talia said. "And I will do what I can to gather more information and pass it along."

"Get back safe," I told her and reached out to pull her into an embrace. "Thank you for everything you've done for us."

"Camelot has always been our ally. And I happen to like you, so it would have been a shame to let you die."

I watched her take a few steps back, regarding me with amusement. "Go on, I want to see what you can do."

No pressure.

Gethin relinquished his grip on my arm to give me room to work. I etched a circle in the air and pictured my mother's sitting room in my mind. It wasn't the politest thing to do, but we needed to reach her as quickly as possible. With any luck, Emerys would be with her, and we wouldn't have to repeat our tale more than once.

The spell snapped into place. I grabbed Taron and Gethin by the arms and hauled them through. I barely caught a glimpse of Talia smirking before the portal closed.

"What happened to you?" My mother's words carried a hint of alarm.

I opened my mouth to ask how she knew something had gone awry when I glanced down at my clothes and realized for the first time they were covered with grit, sweat, and sported several acid-related holes.

"We went dragon hunting and found some things."

"A dragon it would appear," Emerys said from behind us.

"A far less friendly one," Taron noted.

"Does this have something to do with our recent technological troubles?"

"We may have found one of the original members of the Syndicate," I explained. "Goes by the name Vilmar. No idea if that was his name back then or not. We managed to grab some artifacts from his lair before that nasty red mist did us in."

"Gethin bore the brunt of it," Taron added.

"I'm okay. Well, at least I can breathe now."

Emerys moved to stand in front of her apprentice, checking him over, and brushing hair off of his forehead to check for signs of fever or burns. "You should have a full medical evaluation."

"Really, I don't think that's necessary."

"I could make it a royal decree if you like," my mother noted with a cheeky note to her voice.

I turned to my friend and said, "I promise we aren't going anywhere without you. Please take care of yourself."

He nodded and headed for the door. I caught my mother tap something on the side of one of her chairs and when the door opened, a guard appeared and looped one arm through Gethin's to help him to the infirmary. I sunk into the other free chair and rubbed my face.

"I know I am not entitled to know your kingdom's decisions as I am not one of its citizens, but I am curious as to what Camelot's response will be," Taron addressed my mother, his tone formal and clipped.

"This threat isn't going away. We all thought they disbanded centuries ago, and we were wrong. We need to face it head on."

"Well, we've got a place to start. We just left Vilmar in his creepy cave. Surely there's more we could glean from him there."

"No. He'll have destroyed anything else of use," Taron answered.

"Then where do we go from here?"

"I wish I knew the answer. I have only ever met with him in the cave."

But there had to be a way we could track him down. As if on cue, metal warmed against my chest. I reached up and pulled the compass from beneath the fabric of my shirt. It appeared to glow as if it was reflecting the sun. I closed my fingers around it and took a slow breath inward.

Show me what I'm missing.

I wasn't entirely sure that the compass could give clues without me standing in the Crystal Cave, but I didn't have the motivation to make another trek there just yet. The smooth surface of the compass changed, becoming dented and no longer round. Wait, that seemed wrong. I opened my eyes and looked down again. The compass was no longer as it had been. It's circumference was elongated and tapered to a more triangular shape with a band of green in the middle.

"Please tell me I'm not the only one seeing this," I said.

"I think it's showing us what you need to locate next in your journey," Emerys answered.

"It looks like a shield," my mother noted.

How on earth was a shield supposed to help us find a centuries-old dragon hell-bent on bringing down every kingdom and ignite war? I broke contact with the compass, and it rippled back into its proper form, except a tiny green gem still twinkled in the center. When I brushed a fingertip across it, the room around me vanished and all I saw was Talia lying prone on the ground, a pool of blood expanding beneath her.

SEVEN

"Talia!"

The princess' name was out of my mouth before I realized what was happening. My mother's sitting room came back into view, and I found Taron, my mother, and Emerys watching me with worried expressions. I reached for Taron.

"I—I just saw ... I think she's in danger."

"She went back to share what transpired with our parents and advisors," Taron reminded me.

"I know, but the compass showed me ... God, I hope it's just a vision of what might happen."

"Tell me." His eyes locked on mine.

I wasn't sure I could form the words to convey the horror I'd seen. "She was on the floor. She wasn't moving ... and there was a lot of blood."

"Was she in human or shifted form?"

"Human. Why's that matter?"

"We are more susceptible in our unshifted form."

"Then why are we standing here talking? Someone needs to warn her."

I grabbed Taron by the arm, tugging him towards the door. He resisted my forward momentum and produced a cell phone. "Simply because you saw something dire doesn't mean it is real."

My fingers itched to trace a circle in the air and portal us there, but I realized I had never been to his castle and had no frame of reference. Still, he appeared awfully calm about the fact his sister and the heir apparent to his family's crown could be in mortal danger. Dragons were long-lived and power-ful, but even they weren't unkillable.

I watched as Taron raised the phone to his ear. I was vaguely aware of the sound of the line ringing on the other end. His face fell as the call went to voicemail. Clearly not the outcome he'd been hoping for. He stowed the device and moved to open the door.

"You may be right. Even if she were in confer-ence with our parents, she would take my call, especially knowing that Vilmar and the Syndicate is out there."

"Flying will take too long," I noted.

"I may be able to assist in that regard," Emerys said, stepping up beside me. I caught the glint of the gold necklace around her neck. She brushed the tip of one finger against the metal and smiled. It was a wistful expression, almost like she longed to be elsewhere. She raised her hand in the air and in moments, a portal popped into existence. I studied the space within the magic circle's confines. It was a grey stone corridor with floors that looked almost wooden. I picked up on the hint of smoke in the air and my heart beat faster against my ribs.

I caught Taron give Emerys an amused look. "One day, I may have to hear the tale of how the Queen's advisor knows about the passage beneath the dragon throne room."

"And one day, I might share that." She made a shooing gesture. "Go. Save your kin."

I grabbed Taron's hand and yanked him through the portal. Enough chatting about things that didn't matter. We had a princess to save. The moment my feet hit the wooden planks on the other side, I stopped. I had no fucking idea where to go next.

"This way," Taron said, urging me onward and away from the portal.

I cast one last glance over my shoulder as the portal winked out of existence. I caught the worry on Emerys' face before she vanished. The corridor ahead of us looked interminable as we rushed. Taron finally grabbed my hand and pulled me sideways towards a dark expanse of wall. I tensed, expecting to slam into stone, but there was nothing to hit. When I opened my eyes, we were standing at the bottom of a stairway.

"False walls," he explained, as he started up the stairs.

"You could have given me some warning," I grumbled.

He just shrugged in response. As we moved higher, I could pick up the sound of voices. They were muffled, but I thought one sounded like Talia. Well, that was a good sign. She couldn't have a conversation if she was dead. But that didn't mean danger wasn't lurking somewhere in the ether.

We stopped at a roughhewn door. Its hinges were worn with age, and what appeared to have been a handle that had rotted away. Or maybe it had never been there. I watched as Taron pressed his fingers into what looked to be gouges in the wood.

The door swung outward silently to reveal the sweeping interior of the throne room.

It's what I'd always imagined Camelot would look like with high windows framed by luxurious satin curtains that fell to the floor. The floor was polished stone and the two thrones that sat ahead of us looked like they were a good eight feet tall, covered in thick deep purple fabric. Much taller than the average human. I found myself trying to assess if they were wide enough to accommodate a dragon in shifted form.

"You aren't listening to me," Talia argued.

"We hear you. But what proof do you have?" a deep male voice replied.

I couldn't see Talia's face, but I heard her foot-steps pacing against the smooth stone. "When have I ever needed to prove anything to you?"

Beside me, Taron eased the door shut and made a move to make his presence known. "I am the proof," he called, rounding the far edge of the thrones.

His surprise reveal left me no choice except to trail after him, slinking out of the shadows like I wasn't meant to be there. I rounded the edge of the dais where the thrones sat to find two people who couldn't have been anyone but Talia and Taron's parents. They shared the same coloring and natural beauty as their children. It appeared Taron's intense gaze came from his mother while Talia's lithe frame was all their father.

"What is the meaning of this?" the Queen asked, pointing to me. The sleeves of her dress, which matched the throne's coloring, flared from her elbows and the hem brushed the floor as she moved. It covered her feet so completely I couldn't have even guessed if she was in heels or flats.

"Uh, sorry not sure if I'm supposed to bow or something, but honestly we don't have time for formalities," I blurted before pointing to Talia. "She's in danger."

The King sat forward in his seat. He wore a pale gold linen shirt underneath a fitted plum-colored velvet vest and tight grey trousers that tapered into thigh-high boots. "What sort of danger?"

"The kind where Taron has to step back into being next in line to the crown."

"Morgan had a vision and Talia is not safe here," Taron agreed. "I swear to you the Syndicate is alive and well. I have seen it firsthand."

"Even if they were still operating, why would they attack Talia?" the Queen argued.

"Because their aim has always been to sow

chaos and discord," Taron said. "They distrust the monarchy. Assassinating the Crown Princess would do a great deal to destabilize our people."

"They're the ones who took down Camelot's network. The Seelie's too," I explained, beginning to pace. "I know you don't know me, but your son and daughter trust me. And I trust them. Talia helped save my friend's life today after what Vilmar did. I have to believe that you want this threat gone as much as I do."

"I saw the technology that they used to cripple our allies and our enemies," Taron added. "It is unmistakable. We must get all of you out of here now."

"I'm not going anywhere. Let that bastard try and take me out," Talia said, her voice all bravado.

Part of me couldn't blame her. She was a warrior and thought herself indestructible. "My magic led me here for a reason and I'm pretty damn sure it's not so you could die a martyr."

"Enough talking. We need to go," Taron urged and reached for his mother's hand to escort her off the dais.

Commotion beyond the closed doors to the throne room drew my ear. Every muscle in my body tensed as I picked up on the clang of metal on metal.

My heart thudded against my ribs as I turned to face the entrance.

"You said you're safer as dragons, yeah?" I called to Taron.

"There isn't room for four of us in here," he replied.

"Then I suggest we run," I said.

"I will not run away," the Queen replied.

"Mother, please," Taron pleaded.

"Take Talia and get somewhere safe. Let them come and try to take our crowns. They will fail."

As the doors slammed open, I realized that no one was realistically going anywhere. They were all too stubborn and too proud to run from a fight. So, I did the only thing I could, I pressed the pad of my right index finger to the sapphire around my wrist and Excalibur sprang to life.

I expected Vilmar to be leading the charge, but the three brutes who thundered into the room were young, no more than twenty or thirty years old by the looks of them. They all bore the Syndicate's brand on their bare muscular biceps. Well, if the King and Queen needed more proof that their greatest domestic threat was real, they had it.

"You dare enter this castle without invitation," the King boomed, standing to his full height.

"His assault on our Master is invite enough," one of the intruders argued, jutting his chin toward Taron.

"Your Master tried to murder my friends," I replied. "Your little plan to start a war fell apart, too. So, why not slink back to the shadows for another few hundred years?"

The one who'd spoken first turned to glare at me. I could feel the disdain for my very being rolling off of him. "How dare you speak to me."

"I'm a princess too, you arsehole and I'll speak to whoever the fuck I want," I snapped back.

In my peripheral vision, I watched Talia take a step closer to me. "Maybe don't antagonize the intruders," she stage whispered.

"They came looking for a fight. I'm just giving them what they want." I leveled the sword blade at the man in front of me. "Because in case you missed the memo, I'm Morgan Pendragon and these are my allies. You fuck with one of us, you get all of us."

The man standing before me took a step back, as if my words had physically wounded him. I had just enough warning to hit the floor before he opened his mouth and a stream of flames hurtled towards me. I went into a roll, popping up on one knee in front of the Queen. The fabric on the edge of the King's throne smoldered.

"You are unconventional. But you had one thing right. Our kingdoms are allied. I think it's about time we acted like it."

I pushed myself to my feet, positioning myself in front of her, sword held outward. More jetties of flame came straight for my face, and I was too slow in raising Excalibur to deflect the attack. Heat rushed past me, but I didn't feel the searing pain of burns. I looked up to find Talia holding the flame in her outstretched palm. She contemplated it for a moment, as if it truly fascinated her before she lobbed it back at the offending intruder. It hit him squarely in the chest and his skin sizzled, taking on a slight reddish hue. Not enough to hinder him, but still uncomfortable enough to distract him momentarily.

We needed to find a way to corral them, so they couldn't just keep attacking. My vision momentarily blurred as I felt a shift in the air around us. I could swear everything took on a gauzy red tinge for a moment. They were trying to poison us. These guys were really starting to irritate me even more than they had already.

We needed to neutralize the mist. Burning it

away had worked when Talia cured Gethin, but that risked serious damage to the space around us. I looked around, hoping something would spark an idea.

'Starve them.'

Nim's voice echoed in my mind, as if she were standing beside me and whispered the words in my ear. They didn't make sense in the context. Not at first. As another of our assailants conjured a ball of flame, I understood what it meant. We needed to eliminate the air that allowed them to create the flames in the first place. Would it have the side effect of snuffing out the mist, too? It was a risk I was going to have to take.

I knelt down, pressing the flat of Excalibur's blade to the stone flooring. It was cool to the touch. Logically, I knew it wasn't made of ice, but the texture and temperature were enough to spark an idea in my mind. Also, down this low, the mist wasn't nearly as cloying. I turned my thoughts inward, tugging on the kernel of my magic settled deep within my core.

Help me protect them.

The stones beneath my fingers shimmered as thin veins of ice spider-webbed out from my finger-tips. The surface turned into a skating rink and everywhere the magic touched the mist, it froze into tiny red ice formations. I could feel the dark magic push against my own intent to keep it contained, but I pushed onward. The frost zipped up the walls and ceiling, coating the entire room in a thin layer of ice. The mist turned temporarily inert, giving me the time I needed to hinder their ability to kill us in more conventional ways. I closed my eyes, trying to envision what I wanted my magic to do. A literal black hole appeared in my mind's eye, spinning an infinite spiral of nothingness.

In my left hand, Excalibur's hilt warmed against my skin, and I opened my eyes to find the entire sword pulsating with a greenish glow. I lifted the hilt and for a moment, my vision tunneled and all I could see was the strange shield the compass had become in my mother's sitting room.

I was vaguely aware of surprised shouts around me as the sword pulled me forward, the point of its blade drawn to the center of the room. I followed the weapon's lead and allowed it to slam point first into the floor. The greenish glow pulsed twice more and all of a sudden, my lungs burned from lack of oxygen.

That worked better than expected.

My vision greyed out within seconds as the

severe lack of air started to take a toll on my body. I felt someone grab me from behind. I thrashed weakly against them as the ice began to fade from the walls and floor. Maybe it was my vision, but it looked as though the mist wasn't getting worse. Had I actually prevented a royal assassination with some bravado and ice magic?

My feet bumped along something uneven, and my lungs rejoiced at the fact wherever we were had air. My vision sorted itself out a moment later and I found Gethin standing on a step below me supporting my weight.

"How'd you ...?" I couldn't finish my question.

"Emerys figured you could use some help." He looked almost disappointed.

"They're getting away," Talia shouted from a step above me.

I turned to see Taron blocking the exit. The King and Queen appeared safe beside him. I sagged against Gethin's outstretched arm.

"Don't worry, I've got a way to track them," Gethin said, holding up a small circular device. "It looks like they're heading for the barrier."

EIGHT

Gethin's words took far too long to process in my mind. How the hell did he know where the Syndicate pricks had gone? And how could they have gotten all the way to the barrier in Camelot's territory already? Unless time had gone wibbly wobbly and our exit from the throne room had taken far longer than I realized.

"How?" The single word seemed to sum up the majority of my questions.

"I ran into Avery after I got checked out," Gethin began, starting down the stairs and back into the passage beneath the throne room. I followed him, gripping his arm for balance. The echo of additional sets of footsteps signaled that the royal family was hot on our heels. "I filled her in on what we'd found, and she did a bit of tech magic ... literally ... to latch on to the symbol they brand themselves with."

"How could she know how to access it? Vilmar indicated it was more than just a brand," Taron pointed out.

"Honestly, I didn't quite follow it all. But she said something about the code used to take down the network was also embedded in the magic branding them. So, now we've got this little gadget to track them."

"Who exactly are we tracking?" My balance finally righted itself when we reached the corridor below.

"Uh, whoever it was that unleashed the hack."

Well, that ruled out Vilmar himself. One of the thugs from earlier was a more likely fit. Except they'd all looked too much like the muscle to be intelligent enough to handle something as intricate as taking down two sophisticated systems. Well, it didn't matter. The assassins were members of the Syndicate and headed for the barrier. If they made it through, there was no telling what they might do. They could simply get lost in the crowd back in my world or rendezvous with the bastards in Boston and launch a new attack.

"We need to get there then," I announced.

"Thought you might say that," Gethin said. "But aren't you forgetting something?"

I looked at him, confusion clouding my thoughts. What the hell is he on about? We were both wearing clothes that wouldn't be out of place in London, so that couldn't be it. I brushed a few stray strands of hair from my face with my left and realized the bracelet was gone. Fuck!

"Excalibur!"

I spun on my heel and started back up the stairs.

"It isn't safe to go back." Taron tried to bar my way.

"You don't understand, if it falls into the wrong hands there's no telling what could happen."

"You share a bond with this blade, don't you?" the King asked softly.

"Sort of."

"I was not yet born when it was gifted to your ancestors. But I have studied its magic, and the way those who forged the blade crafted it. So, long as you are truly a Pendragon, it cannot be parted from you. Simply call it using the magic that binds you and it should return to your side."

The panic making the blood rush to my head subsided a little. I took a few slow, steadying breaths and reached out with my magic. I could almost see

Excalibur still stuck in the middle of the throne room, emitting the greenish glow that had sucked all of the oxygen from the room.

Excalibur.

I flexed my left hand and felt the familiar weight and presence of the bracelet nestled against my skin and when I opened my eyes, the jewelry was there, like it had never left. A wave of relief hit me as I held up my hand to make sure it was unscathed.

"You must go," the Queen urged.

"What about you all? They could come back."

"Your people have already found a way to track them by their tainted magic."

"I'm sure Avery would be happy to share what she's come up with," Gethin said.

"I think I'd like to meet this Avery," Talia said. "They wouldn't dare attack me in a neighboring kingdom. Not so soon after breaching our defenses. I would be safer in Camelot."

I appreciated Talia's ability to anticipate her parents' objections. I was only sad I wouldn't be present to see Talia and Avery's introduction.

"As much as I'd love to make those introductions, I don't think we have time for me to portal to the castle and then again out to the barrier."

"I appreciate the offer, but I can make my way to Camelot on my own."

"I am going with Morgan. I may have been misled by Vilmar, but I still possess knowledge that could be useful in tracking them and understanding what they may do next," Taron announced. His loose shirt and tight trousers weren't exactly what most blokes wore around London, but if anyone asked, we could just say he was foreign. It wouldn't be a lie.

"You are venturing into a land not your own," the King noted. "Take care of yourself, son."

"I promise I'll bring him home to you," I vowed, offering a hand to the man standing behind me.

"We have not known each other long, Princess, but I do believe you are a woman of your word."

He clasped my hand between both of his and gave me an encouraging nod. "Travel safely and swiftly, Morgan Pendragon."

Pulling my hand from his, I focused on the empty space ahead of us in the corridor. It was easy to conjure the image of the woods that led from this world back to the one I'd been raised in. The image of the shield flashed through my mind, like a beacon guiding me. Would another knight be at the end of this particular journey as there had been on the last two trips? Part of me hoped that would be the case.

The scent of the forest hit me first as the portal opened. I longed to just head back to Emerys' cabin for a rest and a dip in the lake with Taron. Like we'd done a week ago back when things were normal. Instead, we were off chasing some chaos-loving separatists hell-bent on upending civilized society.

"Tell my mother I'll be back soon." I addressed Talia before stepping through the portal.

I stayed off to one side as Taron and Gethin moved through. It was then that I noticed Gethin carrying the bag with the items we'd taken from Vilmar's cave. I gestured to the circular disk in his hand. "Well, what's it say? Did we beat them here?"

He tilted his head as he studied the device. "She said if it blinks red, they're far away and if it's green then they're right on top of us."

It was an unhelpful deep amber color and wasn't blinking at all. "You said that it signaled they were coming this way before you showed up. How long ago was that?"

"Ten minutes maybe?"

"Even flying here, they'd need to take at least twenty."

"But couldn't they just portal here like we did?"

"While dragons can travel through others' portals, we don't possess the aptitude to create them easily ourselves. We are much more comfortable in the air."

"This is the only place they can get through," Gethin noted. "And we know that they have contacts beyond the barrier. It stands to reason they'd be heading there to regroup."

"So, we should just go through and wait on the other side. We know where it leads," I urged.

Just then, the tiny light flipped to a blinking green and a large shadow fell over us in the afternoon sky. Looking up, I saw the belly of a massive dragon. I couldn't explain how I knew it was Vilmar. The scales, while still shiny had an aged look to them and it moved more slowly than the second beast overhead.

"I think we beat them here," I said, gauging our surroundings.

If we could stop them before they made it through the barrier then all of this could be over. We could bring them to justice for the attack on Camelot and the assassination attempt on the Dragon royal family. The second dragon, which had an alluring silver tint to its scales let out a burst of flame as it circled overhead.

"Come on down here and fight us you cowards," I yelled.

"You really need to learn not to antagonize the enemy," Taron muttered.

"Normally, I would agree with you, but I think she has a point," Gethin offered. "At least I'm assuming you're trying to draw them to the ground to stop them from going through."

"It would solve all our problems. Besides, don't they have to land to get through anyway?"

"Uh, I'm not actually sure," Gethin admitted. "I don't know much about the properties of the barrier. I tried studying up on it after our last trip, but there's surprisingly little written about it."

"It is a gateway that divides this realm from the one you were raised in, yes?" Taron asked, not taking his eyes off the circling creatures.

"As far as we know, yeah," I answered, feeling the muscles in my neck tense as I, too, tried to keep track of both beasts.

"Simply because you have not tested whether it extends skyward, doesn't mean it wouldn't. It may be a naturally occurring phenomena in which case, it would have adapted to suit anything that could pass through."

"If that's true, how come we don't have things like drones and aircraft crashing through from the other side then?" I challenged.

"Because they're not magical."

Oh, right. Stupid question.

"Then assuming they can just fly through, why haven't they?" Gethin asked.

"My guess is, they aren't sure what we're going to do," Taron replied.

"Can you, I don't know, convince them to come down dragon to dragon?"

"They aren't going to listen to anything I have to say."

Well, if they weren't coming down on their own and I wasn't keen to be up in the air dealing with them, where one wrong move could send me falling to my death, I needed something else to get them back on solid ground. A net of some sort would be rather useful. The dragons we'd faced in the throne room hadn't been keen on the ice I'd created. So, maybe I could use that again.

Overhead, the silver dragon made a wide arc and let out another burst of flame. I heard Gethin's sharp intake of breath, and I turned to make sure he was unharmed.

"They're testing the barrier with fire." A look of wonder and admiration were painted on his features.

Maybe that was a good thing. If they were focused on the barrier they wouldn't be expecting my attack. I raised my hands, doing my best to block everything else out and imagined my fingers weaving together a net of tiny, icy tendrils. My fingertips stung as the hint of limes tickled my nose. It was working, but slowly. I longed for Emerys or Jules and that connection we'd shared in the office fight. I'd felt so strong—connected to them and their power.

"Give me your hands," I called, reaching out to the two men beside me.

Without question both responded, and I visualized the net expanding exponentially, until it was big enough to pull the dragons from the sky. I shivered as the ice from the spell tried to cling to me.

"I'm going to need a little help getting this thing skyward," I said, my teeth starting to chatter from the cold.

Somehow, without having to explain what I'd envisioned happening, the three of us moved in unison, lifting our arms upward. The net shot up like a rocket, snapping tight around the two dragons. Tiny blue veins of ice sparkled against their scales. Vilmar shuddered at the contact and lost a few feet of altitude. His companion, however, remained airborne.

"Focus on Vilmar. He's weakened from earlier," Taron instructed, his tone commanding.

"What about his friend?"

"If he falls, his companion will come for him. He is revered by his followers. They will not abandon him."

With a waving motion, I directed the spell to pull free of the silver dragon, draping tightly over Vilmar's back and wings. It pressed down against his body, and he lost a few more feet until he started spiraling toward the ground. I skittered back to avoid him crashing on me. His wings broke through tree branches, sending leaves and bits of wood splintering out of the flora around us. He hit the ground with a meaty thud that reverberated throughout the forested area and shook the ground beneath my feet.

As Taron predicted, the silver dragon landed at Vilmar's side. With sharp claws, it dug at the net, trying to free its master. Puffs of smoke plumed from the sides of its mouth as it struggled to undo my magic.

"You got them down, now what?" Gethin whispered.

His words were enough to draw the younger dragon's attention. In one fluid motion, he shifted from beast back into a man with short-cropped dark hair, threaded with veins of silver. His eyes were a murky grey blue, and his skin was much lighter than I'd have expected.

"Release him," he demanded.

"You're mental if you really think that would happen."

"I will end you where you stand, witch."

"That's Princess witch to you, prick."

Underneath the ice net, Vilmar shifted back to his human form, curled up on his side and shivering against the cold. The mark between his shoulder blades glittered in the dying sunlight. The other man glanced from me to his fallen mentor and back like he was judging which of us would be faster. He rose, belching a great ball of flame that he sent hurtling straight for my chest.

Not for the first time today, Taron shielded me from the blast. He spun, his back muscles trans-forming into wings again in a partial shift. I could see the tension in his jaw as he exerted himself, holding both forms at once. The heat died down and when we turned. Vilmar and his accomplice had vanished, the sound of their footsteps hurrying through the underbrush the only hint that they'd made it through the barrier.

NINE

I didn't give Gethin or Taron a second thought. I just started running full tilt through the brush and trees. They could catch up to me. After all, I had no evidence to believe they had to be with me to get through the barrier. My lungs burned as I pushed myself to move faster, barely making it over a fallen log without falling flat on my face. But I could see the terrain ahead of me shifting, flattening out as the trees vanished, replaced by open fields and hills.

"Morgan, wait up," Gethin called from behind me.

Except I kept going. Vilmar and his companion had both been in human form and stark naked. Even if they beat us through the barrier, they wouldn't make it far in modern day Ireland in that state. With any luck, tourists would spot and detain them long enough for us to make it there and haul their arses back through. But then, luck hadn't seemed to be on our side for much of this adventure.

I only stopped running when I reached the foot of the incline that signaled the change in realms. I bent double, hands pressed to my knees as I gasped for breath. I scanned my surroundings, but saw nothing that would signal Vilmar and his friend were nearby. I reached into my pocket for the tracker only to realize Gethin had taken it back. Damn it. Two pairs of heavy footsteps thundered behind me and a moment later, Gethin and Taron materialized from thin air. I watched Taron look around in wonder at the sudden shift in scenery.

"It is so different," he marveled.

I thought I heard Gethin mutter something akin to 'amateur' under his breath as he readjusted his pack and walked over to me. "So, where'd they go?"

Several loud shouts echoed from over the rise in front of us. As a group, we took off and crested the hill in time to see two teenagers sprawled on the grass. A third teen, a young woman with jet black hair, crouched between their bodies, shaking them vigorously. As we approached, I could see that the boys had been stripped to their boxers. Apparently, dragons didn't need undergarments. I noticed bruising on one of the boy's cheeks and a cut on the other's arm.

"Hi there," I said, approaching the girl slowly with my hands held out by my sides to signal I wasn't a threat.

She spun to face me, holding a can of mace at the ready. "Where the fuck did you lot come from?"

"Just over the ridge. We heard the commotion. Can you tell us what happened?"

I knelt down beside her and felt for a pulse in the boys' wrists. They were strong and steady. So, at least Vilmar and his accomplice didn't kill them outright. Just took their clothes.

"We were just hanging, you know. Having a smoke, and these two blokes came out of nowhere," she answered, gesturing in the direction Taron, Gethin, and I had come. "The skinnier one just hit Bernie in the face and demanded he take off his clothes. What a damn perv."

"Did you happen to see which way they went?" Taron crouched beside me, his tone gentle.

The girl dried her eyes and pointed in the direction of the car park and the main tourist attraction of the area. Part of me wanted to run after them and the way Taron's leg muscles tensed, as if he were about to spring into the air to take flight, told me he had similar thoughts. But we couldn't just leave these poor kids without help.

"Dial the police, tell them you and your mates were assaulted. They'll provide the help you need." After a moment I added, "What were your mates wearing?"

"Jeans and Shamrock Rovers jerseys."

She nodded and reached into her pocket for her phone. She started to dial the emergency line, but stopped. "You three came from the same way as those crazies."

"Yeah, we're trying to catch them. They're not well," I said.

"I thought they were going to kill us. The skinny one looked half mad."

"You're safe now," I said and stood. I turned to my companions. "Come on, we might be able to see which way they went and catch them."

I walked slowly, waiting just long enough to hear the girl connect with the police before I picked up the pace. I fell into step beside Taron who walked with such determination one might mistake him for having a clue of where we were going.

"You aren't mad we stopped to help them, are you?" I hated having to ask the question.

"Of course not. They were innocents. They did not ask for any of this."

"You think they realized it would be too conspicuous to shift here and that's why they stole their clothes, so they could blend in?" Gethin asked.

"Given how long Vilmar has lived, I would not be surprised if this wasn't his first trip through the barrier. After all, as Morgan said, there were Syndicate operations established in this world. They had to come from somewhere."

"I think the net spell I used must have hurt him more than any of us realized. I doubt they'll be able to get to Boston to regroup with their mates there."

"So, what next?" Taron looked around at the smattering of cars parked in neat spaces.

My first thought was to portal back to London and regroup there. But if Vilmar and company were sticking local, at least for the time being, we needed to be here, too. I scanned the small crowds of people, assessing who might be willing to give us a lift at least into Dublin.

"Uh, Morgan, I think you ought to take a look at this," Gethin said, holding up the tracking device.

It had gone solid amber again, but there was a new depression at its center, as if it was meant to hold something. The compass warmed against my breastbone.

"Give it here."

He passed it over and I tugged the compass over my head, slotting it into the depression in the tracker. I watched in stunned silence as the tracker melded with the compass, the amber light shimmering and reappearing on the outside of the compass. Handy.

No one around seemed like they could spare the space for three extra bodies, and I didn't want to push Taron to shift in an unfamiliar place. After all, I didn't know if dragons faced similar challenges with feeling cut off from their magic like witches did if they were away from their birth origins too long.

"It's at least an hour to Dublin," I announced.

"And why do we wish to go there?" Taron asked.

"Because it's the nearest major city and if they need to get in touch with their counterparts in America, they're going to need better reception than the shitty service out here," I answered. "Now come on, we've got a ride ahead of us."

I led the way to the small one-room building selling admission to the area and picked up a printed bus schedule. Double checking the time, I tapped on the glass partition. A bored looking bloke looked up from his phone.

"Can I help you?"

"Yeah. Couple of things. First, you didn't happen to see two blokes come by here not long ago, did you? Might have been running like they wanted out of here fast?"

He shook his head. "Nope."

Well, that didn't surprise me. "And do you sell bus tickets to Dublin?"

He nodded, only half interested. "What time?"

"The one that leaves in ten minutes," I answered and passed over a credit card.

He returned the card, handed over the tickets, and gave me directions to the bus stop. Now I just had to hope we didn't lose too much ground in our dragon-shaped pursuit.

My head knocked against the window as the bus hit a pothole, jolting me from a restless doze. I looked around, momentarily disoriented by my surroundings. But the dragon chase and scuffle at the barrier came flooding back to me as I sat up and my shoulders gave an ache in protest that I'd moved. Somehow, we'd managed to secure the single row of three seats at the very back of the bus when we'd boarded. Gethin sat wedged between Taron and I, his glasses hanging precariously off the tip of his nose as he snored softly. I wasn't surprised he'd fallen asleep. After being nearly poisoned to death, he hadn't exactly had much chance to recover.

Taron sat at the other window, gaze focused on every passing car, tree, and structure. I nudged Gethin in the ribs and he stirred enough for me to maneuver around him and gesture for him to switch seats. He gave a cough as he straightened his glasses and took the spot I vacated.

"It's really not that different from Albion," I started, drawing Taron's attention away from the window.

"And yet it *feels* different," he said softly.

He didn't need to explain what he meant. It was a sensation I'd encountered on my first trip through the barrier into Albion from this world. But then again, I'd been headed somewhere I was meant to be and not a completely new realm. He turned so he faced me more directly.

"I must admit I am not used to feeling like such a stranger in my own skin. Logically, I know my magic is still there and I need only reach for it. But I think perhaps Vilmar and his accomplice failed to shift because they felt this same disconnect with their shifted form; from the essence of what their magic feels like in that form."

Well, that answered one question that had been kicking around in my head. "I spent my whole life feeling that way. Your magic's not gone. You can still access it, but it might ... I don't know, hurt a bit?"

"Then let's hope we don't have a need for me to make that change."

"If you're right and Vilmar is afraid to shift. Or he doesn't think he can, at least not right away, that gives us a fighting chance of tracking them down."

Then again, reports of dragons tearing through the Irish countryside would have been like a giant neon sign to guide us, too. I glanced down at the compass bouncing against my chest with every bump the bus made. It had changed from that solid amber to a sort of pea-green color, which I hoped meant we were at least headed in the right direction.

"I don't think I ever said thank you for coming along on this trip with me."

"It's my honor to do it." He leaned in close. "And as I said before, I had hoped one day I could accompany you on such a quest."

"I would like to say they don't tend to be so life and death, but that would be a lie. It seems the universe is out to prove it can kick my arse whenever it wants."

"Ah, but you keep getting back up, stronger each time."

"Why do you think they went dormant for so long?" Gethin asked, sending the topic of conversation veering back toward the men we were chasing.

"Maybe there was too much attention on them, and they wanted to go into hiding?" I said, looking at him.

"They were responsible for a lot of the uprisings and upheaval in the realm for hundreds of years and then all of a sudden they just stopped. That doesn't make tactical sense. It's almost like their focus or their drive disappeared."

"Maybe they lost more than just a drive to sow chaos," Taron said quietly.

The furrow of his brow drew my full focus. "What's that mean?"

"I was obviously not alive yet, nor were my parents or my grandparents, but there was talk of something like a purge. The King, growing fed up with the constant attacks, hunted down every suspected Syndicate member and sympathizer ...

and had them executed. Even if they couldn't prove they'd done anything wrong."

"Well, obviously not everyone," Gethin muttered.

"I didn't think the monarchy was that ruthless," I noted.

"Dragons by nature are noble creatures. At least the majority. However, there are those that give our kind a bad reputation, stealing young girls as trophies and the like."

"Every fairy tale has to have some truth to it," I pointed out.

"But generally, we honor and respect life. We are also keenly aware that we have a duty to protect those who cannot defend themselves. And at the time, the Syndicate grew in strength because it fed on fear. To keep our kingdom safe, my ancestors had to take drastic action. I see how now what he did could have stoked the flames of fear as well."

"And if I'm Vilmar or any of his other mates who managed to survive, then I would want to lay low for a while, too. Maybe even come back in a new form to the fit the times," I continued. "There's always going to be people who feel marginalized and think that joining a cult is going to give them purpose."

"Dublin," the bus driver announced, and the vehicle came to a screeching stop.

I jolted forward out of my seat and Taron barely caught me before I tumbled to my knees. As quickly as possible, we gathered our packs and disembarked. I studied the street signs around us and realized just as the bus pulled away, I had no fucking idea where we were or where to go next.

"If they were running, they would indeed want to try and lay low upon arrival," Taron said, pointing to a sign on an overhang across the street. "If I were them, I would seek lodging for the night."

I led the way across the street and approached the four-story building nestled in between two shops. The sign in the window noted it was a bed and breakfast costing fifty euros a night. Not bad. I'd barely pulled the door open when I felt a sharp pain in my chest. I looked down to find the compass glowing a vivid green.

"Think we're on the right track," I announced and tapped the compass. Score one for dragon intuition and magical tracking devices.

I sucked in a breath and eased the door the rest of the way open. My muscles tensed as we crossed the threshold. My mind conjured up an image of Vilmar waiting for us and my right index finger found the sapphire on Excalibur, transforming the object into a blade. The cock of a gun threw me off guard as I stepped inside to find an older woman with light grey hair in a bob and wearing a tartan sweater leveling a shotgun at my chest.

"No one brings weapons in my house, girlie!" the woman shouted.

I felt Gethin and Taron step up behind me, each making it clear with a simple touch that they had my back.

I tried not to panic as I processed her words. Weapon. Fuck! I shifted Excalibur back into bracelet form, but that only angered the woman more.

"Deceptive little thing."

"Look, Ma'am, we don't mean you any harm. We're just looking for some blokes who might have come through here."

"No one's come through in days." She didn't lower the gun.

I was at a loss for what else to say to convince this woman we meant no harm. And I wasn't going to risk pushing Taron to shift if he wasn't comfortable.

"Christ, Gran, put the bloody gun away!" a young woman's voice shouted from behind us. "They're supposed to be here!"

TEN

The woman's words caught me off guard. Someone knew we were coming? But we hadn't known we'd end up here until a few minutes ago when we got off the bus. We hadn't told anyone we were even headed to Dublin before heading through the barrier. The tiny hairs on the backs of my arms stood on end in warning. Still, I took my eyes off the older woman who continued clutching the shotgun defensively and turned to see a woman no more than twenty years old with copper toned hair done in a plait mid-way down her back standing at the foot of the stairs holding a cloth to the side of her face. She wore a simple black skirt and pale green three-quarter length top. Her eyes were a vivid green to match the shirt. I could see drips of blood that had soaked into the cloth.

"Uh, you were expecting us?"

She pulled the cloth away from her face to show a nasty cut below her eye that still wept. She was going to have a nasty bruise, too. "Well, the two crazies demanding shelter without paying for it were a bit of a giveaway."

"But she said ... " Gethin began.

"Gran was just trying to protect me."

"Aye. Still have a mind to use this," the older woman behind me grumbled, but the clank of metal against wood suggested she'd at least set it down.

"You turned them away, why?" Taron asked.

"Bad vibe," the young woman answered. "And I don't know ... call it intuition or something, but I knew they weren't to be trusted. It's why the skinny one hit me I think."

I immediately flashed to the poisoned claws Vilmar had sported in his cave. "This might sound weird, but uh, did he have fingers or claws when he hit you?"

"Not weird. They were definitely fingers."

That's a relief.

I wasn't sure I had it in me to try and combat whatever poison had nearly killed Gethin without

Talia's assistance. "We need to know where they went."

"The quiet one looked like he was in a bad way," the older woman offered. "My guess is they went looking for a doctor."

I glanced at Taron. "Does that track for you?"

"It would be dangerous. Seeking help from strangers in a new place. But if Vilmar was injured badly enough, yes he probably would seek medical attention."

"I keep forgetting this isn't his first trip through," I admitted and turned back to the wounded woman on the staircase. We needed some allies, or at least a place to rest for a little while and regroup. I could reach out to Avery's FBI contacts in America and see how things had gone with the man they'd arrested. And maybe get something to eat.

"You wouldn't happen to have a couple of rooms for rent, would you?"

"You keep that sword of yours put away, lass, and I might have a room or two," the woman's Gran answered.

"I really didn't mean to do that," I apologized again. "But it sort of has a mind of its own at times and it prefers me alive and breathing, so pointing a gun at me made it jumpy."

"You talk like it's sentient," the young woman on the stairs said, descending so that she was level with me.

The thought that these women had no clue about magic hit me like a ton of bricks. Had we inadvertently managed to put even more mundane lives at risk? My jaw went slack as I tried to come up with a way to explain a magical sword that wouldn't sound mental.

"I don't know about sentient," I began, feeling a sharp pain shoot up my left arm. Apparently, words could wound even an inanimate object. *Brilliant.* "Uh ... We're still getting to know each other."

"Rory, you're making the lass twist herself in knots," Gran muttered.

Rory 's cheeks flushed, accenting the cut even more. "Sorry, I didn't mean to make things awkward. We just have to be careful with who we talk to about this sort of thing."

"What sort of thing?" Gethin asked.

"Well, magic obviously, you dolt," Gran drawled.

Relief washed over me in a warm rush. "Yes, it is absolutely a magic sword and very well could have a literal mind of its own. It's been known to do all sorts of things, like keep me from dying."

"Don't forget that whole thirty year stretch it

embedded itself in stone because you weren't around," Gethin noted jovially.

"What are those blokes after?" Rory asked, redirecting the conversation back to our quarry.

"Chaos," I said with a shrug. "Oh ... and committing a cyber-attack on two separate kingdoms to push them to the brink of war."

"So, you're what, magical bounty hunters?" Gran scoffed, rolling her eyes.

I glanced at my companions before I answered, "Princess actually."

"Dragon," Taron answered with a smirk. "Also, royalty."

"Apprentice to a very powerful witch," Gethin said.

"Well, we best get out the good towels," Gran said. "We've got royalty staying the night. And I suppose you lot ought to just call me Gran, too."

She rounded the counter, plucking two sets of keys off a peg as she went. She gestured for us to follow her up the stairs. I started to trail her and paused as I reached the step where Rory had first appeared. I couldn't shake the feeling we were meant to be here. My gut told me that Rory was going to be the key in finding Vilmar and his accomplice, and maybe the shield that kept plaguing my thoughts too. But she was so young, barely grown really. And given how protective her Gran clearly was, I doubted she'd be allowed to come along this quest unaccompanied.

"I've got some healing skills if you want me to take a look at that cut," Gethin told Rory.

"Don't overexert yourself," I reminded him. "You did almost die this morning."

"Not something I'd be able to forget," he sighed, but probed at Rory's cheek. "Let's get this cleaned off and see what we can do."

Taron and I were left to follow Gran up to the next floor. She stopped at the first door on the right and handed me a silver key. "Old fashioned locks."

"Cheers."

"Your friends will be across the hall."

I barely stifled a snort as I caught her giving Taron serious side eye.

"I assure you, nothing untoward will happen under your roof," he vowed, offering her a deep bow.

"Just don't go slinging any spells around here. Don't need the place burning down."

"Yes, ma'am," I replied as I slid the key into the lock and opened the door.

"Oh, the washroom's at the end of the hall.

There's just the one, so don't dawdle if you have to use it."

I picked up on a high-pitched yelp followed by Gethin apologizing from the first floor. Gran disappeared back downstairs, leaving Taron and I alone on the upper floor. Taron leaned on the doorframe, staring in at the small bed and modest chest of drawers shoved into the far corner of the room. My room in the flat in London with Nim was twice the size.

"So, we find ourselves alone," Taron said, his voice husky.

I spun to face him and found myself positioned perfectly for him to wrap his arms around my waist. He had that look again like he wanted to kiss me. Hell, I doubted either of us could stop if our lives depended on it.

"I don't mean to be a tease, but I could really use some proper sleep. And a decent meal."

I could see the disappointment dance across his features before vanishing. "Yes, we both ought to get some rest while we can. We need to be ready once we've found Vilmar."

I nodded mutely and watched as he walked across the hall. I stayed put long enough to see two beds in the other room. At least he and Gethin wouldn't have to fight for who got the mattress and who ended up sleeping on the floor.

Part of me wanted to check on Gethin after everything he'd been through, but the bed in my own room was alluring. I really did need some proper sleep. I kicked off my boots and laid my jacket at the foot of the bed before climbing beneath the sheets. My eyes grew heavy the moment my head touched the pillow. I nestled against the soft surface and let sleep come for me.

I stood back in Vilmar's cave, the red mist wafting from the floor all around me. I covered my mouth, trying to keep it from burning my lungs, but it didn't seem to help. I looked around for the way out, but it was as if the place had suffered a cave in. Still, as I stood amongst the Syndicate relics, I could hear footsteps against the stone floor.

"Hello?" I called out through a gasp.

No response.

Of course there wasn't one. Coughing, I did my best to follow the sound of the footsteps as they echoed in the enclosed space. I wound my way through a small passageway I wasn't even sure existed in reality and moved into a space where the air was fresh and clean. Light came from large holes in the ceiling overhead, and it cast a soft blue hue over a small figure seated in the middle of the room. Her hair was dark brown with thin veins of gold throughout it that hung like curtains over her face and shoulders. I couldn't see her face, but the lack of curves in her body beneath the simple, yet dirty, brown dress suggested a child. It looked almost like she'd been dressing up as a peasant for one of those medieval fairs.

I coughed a time or two to clear my lungs before saying, "Hi there."

The figure turned and confirmed that they were indeed a little girl. Her eyes were a vibrant shade of green, almost the color of emeralds sparkling in the noontime sun. I couldn't help but search her facial features for any hint that she might be a dragon or worse, fae.

"You're the one searching," she said in a light, high voice.

"Am I?"

"For the bad man and ... for the shield."

In a way it made sense. Vilmar was indeed a bad man and the object we were hoping to find had appeared to be a shield. "Yes, I am. Do you know where I might find either of them?"

Her young face scrunched as she slipped into thought. "Well, I put it somewhere. But I don't remember where."

"You did?" I knelt beside her, taking her right hand in my left. "How'd you get it?"

"I made it."

I did my best to hide my surprise and disbelief that a child could have fashioned a shield. "Maybe I can help you remember where you put it. It's really important that I find it."

She nodded. "If the bad man finds it first, he can hurt a lot of people."

"He already has. He almost took one of my friends from me."

Her bright eyes grew misty with unshed tears. "He took my family away, too."

"I'm so sorry."

"You'll find him, and he won't hurt anyone again?"

"This is his cave, isn't it?" I gestured around us.

"Yes."

I didn't know how to explain to this little girl how I was certain I was dreaming. That this place and conversation couldn't be real. But she looked so certain of the fact she'd made the shield and that if Vilmar got his hands on it, very bad things would happen. I could almost hear Nim's voice in the back of my head telling me to pay attention and that magic works in strange ways. It wouldn't be the first time the universe had given me hints via unusual means.

"What's your name?"

"Laoise"

"And where are you right now?"

Her brow furrowed. "Here."

"In the bad man's cave?"

She nodded. "But you're not. You're far away." She rubbed her eyes. "Very far away. I'm getting sleepy."

It hit me just then that she had brought me to Vilmar's lair. This little girl, Laoise was very much alive, and she was in that cave when we'd been there too. "You rest now, okay? Everything's going to be fine."

"But you have to find it," she urged as her body slumped over and her eyes fluttered shut.

The world around me tilted on its axis as our connection vanished and I went plummeting into the darkness of my own mind.

I sat up in a cold sweat, the room of the B&B coalescing around me. How long had I been asleep? Had Taron ever seen the girl before? Surely, he wouldn't have let her remain captive if he'd realized she was being held against her will. I pushed myself out of the bed and staggered to the door, opening it. I peered across the hall and found the other bedroom closed. Looking out a nearby window I noticed the fading sunlight. I could hear soft voices from below and I descended to the first floor.

Gethin and Rory sat side by side in the eating area, heads pressed intimately together over mugs of what turned out to be hot chocolate. Rory's Gran was nowhere to be seen and neither was her shotgun.

"You look better," Gethin noted, but the way his brow furrowed as he spoke telegraphed the lie. The slight blush on his cheeks also signaled he hadn't expected to be interrupted.

"Had a weird dream. Well, sort of a magical connection with a little girl called Laoise."

"Never heard that name before," he replied.

"I think Vilmar has her locked up in his cave."

"I thought that was just a myth, more of a stereotype," he countered.

"Even those could be grounded in truth."

"You must be hungry," Rory interjected and stood up. "Gethin's made some stew. It's delicious. Can I get you some?"

"If Gethin's made it, I'll take the whole pot."

My friend's cheeks brightened at the compliment. Rory chuckled as she brought out the pot and set it atop a hot plate. She handed me a bowl and let me dish out as much as I wanted.

"You don't like taking compliments, do you?" she teased as she sat back down beside him.

"He's just being modest. I keep telling him that he's got a gift beyond magic with food."

"Having tasted it, I'm not sure I want him to leave when you find what you're looking for," Rory replied with a flirty smile.

"Can I ask how you really knew we were coming?" I pressed, setting my spoon down.

"I told you, the two scary guys showed up and we chased them off." Though she wouldn't meet my gaze.

"Rory, come on. We both know that's a load of bullshit."

"Uh ... Fine, but you can't tell Gran. I think I've been having these visions. It started a couple of months ago."

"When exactly?" Gethin sat up, pushing his glasses into place.

"I don't know. August, I guess. Why? Is that important?"

Gethin rubbed his chin, jaw working as he tried to form words. He looked at me after a moment and said, "Emerys and I were starting to think that perhaps these quests weren't random."

"How so?"

"Well, it seems the universe is bringing you closer to a collection of witches. A sisterhood."

The image I'd first seen in the Crystal Cave of myself leading a host of women into battle flashed through my mind's eye. "So, what, you're saying Rory had been seeing us coming, because the universe thinks I need her?"

"I've heard crazier things," she replied.

A sisterhood of witches. I liked the sound of that.

ELEVEN

I couldn't get Laoise's young face out of my mind as I finished my stew and set the bowl in the sink in the kitchen. Taron still hadn't emerged which worried me. Had he been more worn out than he'd let on? He certainly hadn't appeared to be injured in any way. But seeing his mentor turn on him had to mentally fuck with him.

"So, you're not freaked out that I saw you coming?" Rory asked from behind me.

"After the things I've seen, nah, sounds pretty normal honestly."

"When they started, I thought it was just wishful thinking. Me going on some big adventure. Don't tell Gran, but I've always felt a little stuck here."

"You're what, twenty?" She nodded. "Plenty old enough to be on your own."

Rory shook her head. "Not if you ask her. I think she wants me here until I'm old and craggy like her."

"She have a reason to want to keep you close?"

"I mean, my Dad left when I was little. And Mum died a couple years ago from cancer. I think maybe she's just lonely?"

"I understand that. I lived with my aunt till she died ..." The word choked me, and I looked away from the younger woman. "No, that's not right. She didn't just die. She was murdered."

"Oh, Morgan, I'm so sorry."

"I'd love to say the bastards who did it are facing justice, but they slunk back to their king. I couldn't hunt them down even if I wanted to. Not without risking a war."

"Royal life sounds complicated."

I let out a snort. "You're telling me. And I've only been at this whole princess thing for a few months. Everyone says they'd love to be one, until it actually happens. People are constantly watching your every move and word because you never know when you might do something out of line and people start fighting."

"Gethin told me a little about what happened to

you," she noted. "If you think I can help you on your mission, please take me along."

"Well, so far it seems that the people I meet on these little jaunts tend to come back with me. I'd say the odds are pretty high."

"So, the other bloke ... the hot one."

"Taron?"

"He's like really hot."

"Sometimes literally. He is a dragon and I guess all that fire has to come from somewhere."

"The way he looks at you, it's so intense."

"Is it?"

"Like you're the only thing in the room."

"I think he's just trying to make sure I don't wind up dead. My mother would be rather pissed if that happened since she just got her daughter back."

Rory frowned. "I don't think that's it. I've kind of always been able to feel emotions off people and this is more than just feeling like he has to get you home safely. It's like a fierce devotion."

"I think you're reading into it too much." I hoped she was reading into it too much. That didn't sound like the man I'd spent mornings by the lake with. That sort of serious relationship, especially after what I'd been through, scared me.

"Sorry to interrupt your female bonding," Gethin

called as he walked in carrying the empty stew pot, "But shouldn't we be trying to get in touch with people about our runaway dragons?"

It had been nice, just chatting with Rory, but he was right. We were here for a reason. I pulled out my phone and bit my lip. The international fees were going to be a bitch, but there was no other way around it. I dialed Agent Cartwright's number and waited as the line rang.

"Molly Cartwright," she answered after the third ring.

"Uh, hi, it's Morgan. Morgan le Fey. We met the other day with the—" I rambled.

"Hi, Morgan. Everything okay? I thought Avery said you were heading home."

"Well, we did. But it turns out the people we thought were behind the attack weren't. Right now, we're back on this side in Dublin chasing some of them."

"You hero types really don't get a breather." After a beat she added, "How can we help?"

"I don't know if they'll try to make it to America, but that bastard you arrested the other day, is he still in custody?"

"In a holding cell as we speak. He lawyered up, so we can't talk to him for a while."

That should have given me a sense of relief. But all I could picture was Vilmar or his accomplice dressing up in a suit and pretending to be the bastard's legal representation, and somehow breaking him out of federal custody.

"Just be careful with whoever shows up. He's got connections. This group goes back centuries and they're dragons."

"Oh, that's a new one."

"Creatures have been going through the barrier between realms for ages. I wish it wasn't the case, but here we are."

"Well thanks for the head's up. If you have pictures of the ones you're after, text them over so we can keep an eye out."

"If I can get some, I will."

"How is Avery settling in?"

"Grand. Yeah, seems right at home."

"Good. I had a feeling this was going to be a positive thing for her."

Just then, I picked up the sound of footsteps on the stairs. "I should go."

"Okay. Good luck," she said as I ended the call.

Taron emerged looking rested with his curls pulled back at the nape of his neck into a tight knot. "I appear to have missed a meal."

Gethin glanced at him. "I put some leftovers for you in the fridge. You'll have to reheat it."

"I think I can manage."

Taron looked my way. "Something's wrong."

Rory mouthed the words, 'I told you,' at me.

"I had a dream and connected with a little girl. She claimed she crafted the shield we're after. But Taron, she said she was in Vilmar's cave."

"That's impossible," he scoffed.

"It seemed to be a secret room off of where he kept all the artifacts. I think he's been keeping her prisoner."

Taron's jaw worked as he searched for words. "I hate to believe that he was capable of taking and harming a child. But after the things I've learned about his true nature these last few days, I suppose nothing should surprise me."

"I'm going to get in touch with Jules, see if they can track the girl down. She's scared and alone."

"How are you going to give her directions? Our eyes were closed the whole way," Gethin reminded me.

"I took Talia with me once. She'll know the way there."

It could be a long shot, but it was all we had. I

dialed Jules' number and waited. It rang only once before she picked up.

"Are you back through the barrier yet?"

"No, this is a long-distance call. I need you to do something for me. We've discovered Vilmar was keeping a little girl captive in his lair. You need to take some people and get her out."

"Any idea where we're meant to look?"

"Talk to Talia about finding the cave. She can take you there. It was in a room off of where he kept all his artifacts and Syndicate relics. Hurry, Jules. She's all alone and I'm worried about her."

After a pause on the line, she spoke again. "We will find her. I promise."

"How are things there?" I clung to the sound of my best friend's voice. It was almost like we were just catching up after a long week at work.

"Seems to be back to normal. But both the Queen and Emerys are anxious for you to be home."

"Believe me, I wish I were there right now, too. It feels like I haven't had a moment to breathe since this all began."

"I guess when Nim told us all those stories about you being royalty, she left out the bits where Albion was constantly a world-in-peril, and the princess was always off chasing nutters."

I chuckled. "Yeah, she definitely did not prepare me for all this running around. If she had, maybe I'd have spent more days at the gym."

After a long pause, Jules burst out laughing. "Nah, that's definitely not you."

Her laughter was infectious, and I soon found myself leaning against the edge of the sink in a full-on belly laugh. "Fair point."

It felt so normal to just be having a chat with her, I could almost put the chaos-courting dragons and the mystery shield I was meant to be searching for out of my mind. And then, my phone beeped with another incoming call. That alone was strange enough to halt my laughter. The people who'd normally be calling me at this hour were already on the line, likely listening to the call on the other end or dead. I pulled the phone away from my ear long enough to see Agent Cartwright's number flashing on the screen.

"Jules, I'll have to call you back. Please go find Laoise."

"On it."

My stomach churned as I switched calls. "Agent Cartwright, should I be worried you're calling so soon?"

"I'm afraid so."

My mouth went dry. "What's happened?"

"We've had a breach."

A breach?

"What does that mean?"

"The man you fought to secure the codes to free your kingdom is no longer in FBI custody."

"Someone broke him out?"

"Yes."

"Where's he gone?"

"We were able to track him to a boat in the Seaport before we lost him. He could be headed anywhere."

Something told me that bastard had one destination in mind. "No, he's headed here to Dublin. Somehow, he's figured out the founder of his twisted little club is here, and he wants to see him in the flesh. Or help him disappear. Either way it doesn't matter. He's coming here."

"That's out of our jurisdiction ...." There was a pregnant pause before she added, "It's out of the Authority's purview, too."

There was little chance I'd be going to the Practitioner's Council begging for help. This was a problem I'd have to solve on my own.

"Thank you for the head's up."

"I'm guessing you have a few hours, maybe six or seven at most, before he gets there."

Less if he shifts and flies himself.

"Thanks for the head's up."

"I wish there was more we could do."

"Calling was enough."

I ended the call and my phone nearly slipped from my slack grasp. This little respite time wasn't going to last. Rory and her gun-wielding Gran were about to be dragged into a bigger mess than either of them likely had ever intended.

"You have that look you get when you're trying to figure out how to break bad news," Gethin said, drawing my attention.

"Have we really known each other long enough for you to know my looks?"

He gave me a nervous smile. "I like to think I'm pretty good at reading things like that."

"Better if everyone hears it at one time."

I glanced around the space and realized that Taron and Rory had disappeared. I took a steadying breath and stowed my phone. There was no reason to panic. Rory had said she'd been expecting us. Maybe she was filling him in on what she'd already shared with me. But she'd also seemed interested in him, and I couldn't deny that ignited a bit of jealousy. Taron was my hot dragon.

After a moment, I picked up on Rory's voice coming from an entryway off to the left of the kitchen. I followed the sound of her voice to a small alcove where she stood in front of a table, sketches strewn about. Taron was studying one of them intently. Gethin nearly knocked into me when I stopped.

"Bad news. The bloke Jules, Avery, and I thought we'd handed off to authorities in America has broken out and is on his way here."

Rory's head snapped up. "Here? Like Gran's B&B?"

If he could track Vilmar's movements, it was entirely possible that was the case. "Probably not, but it's better if there's no one around when they do come looking."

"What is our next move?" Gethin asked, following me into the small space.

"Rory was showing me some pieces she had drawn over the last few months," Taron replied. He held up one in pencil and another done in ink.

"Where have I seen that before?" Gethin plucked one of the drawings from Taron's hands and studied it.

"I'm not the best artist. I mean, I dabble. It's a hobby really, but it's been all I can see when I sit to draw lately," Rory explained.

"Since you started having those visions of us coming?" I prompted.

She nodded. "I don't know why, but it's like something is calling to me."

I looked at one of the few drawings with color and my stomach dropped. "The shield."

"Sorry?" Rory's voice was thick with confusion. "I mean, I guess that is what I've been drawing. But why do you sound like you know what it is?"

"Because right before we came here, I had a vision of my own. I'm supposed to find this shield."

"We've been saying that the universe could be orchestrating things to get Morgan the support she needs. Maybe this was its way of preparing you both," Gethin offered.

"He is not wrong. Although, that sort of connection is rare in witches," Taron said almost off-handedly.

"What's that supposed to mean?" Gethin's voice sounded accusatory.

"I simply mean I have heard of that sort of connection being common in dragons or even some fae."

"But we're all magical, aren't we? We all came from the same starting blocks," I noted.

"I suppose, but you and Rory were literally born in different realms. Your magics are tied to different places entirely. And yet, you have been bound together in this quest in such a deep way. I find it fascinating."

"Well, we've got a few hours until our jailbird arrives in the country. We need to find this bloody thing before they realize what's going on and try to take it for themselves."

"Do we have any idea what this shield even does?" Gethin studied another of Rory's drawings.

"Does? It's a shield. It deflects things," Rory answered.

Gethin gave me a knowing look and I exhaled. "Well, the other things we've gathered have had another purpose. This chalice we found has restorative properties and this pendant bestows protection on both the wearer and anyone else they extend it to."

"We need to know more about its origins," Taron said, setting the sketches down.

"All I know is a little girl holed up in Vilmar's cave claims to have crafted it. When or how or where I don't have any idea."

"Are we even sure it's here?" Gethin made a sweeping gesture that I interpreted to mean this realm. "We only came here, because the dragons were coming this way."

"Yes. The two are connected. It's here some-where. We just need to look in the right place."

"I presume people do not simply walk around with magic shields in your realm?" Taron asked, looking at Rory with a serious expression.

"No. Definitely not," she quipped, her expression shifted to one of excitement. "I don't know where it is, but I think I might know who can help us find it."

TWELVE

The excitement in Rory's face was a good sign. It meant we might just get ahead of Vilmar and his goons before they could coordinate. For the first time since coming through the barrier after them, I felt hopeful.

"Well, what are we waiting for?" I prodded.

"I need to let Gran know we're leaving. And to close up for a while, just in case."

"Is there somewhere else she can go? A friend she can stay with?" The older woman still scared me, but I didn't want her getting in the way of vengeful dragons.

"She's got some ladies she does a book club with, but it's going to take a lot to convince her," Rory answered.

"Convince who of what?" Gran's voice came from the open doorway leading from the entryway.

"Those blokes who came through earlier aren't the only ones. We believe more are coming and we've got an errand to run. It's better if you aren't around, in case they track us back here," I explained.

"But this is my home. I'm not running."

"No one is asking you to run. We just want you to be safe," Gethin replied.

"I can protect myself," she scoffed.

Taron straightened to his full height. "I truly mean no disrespect, but I know better than most what they are capable of. You might stand a chance if they remained in human form. But in the confined walls of this place, they wouldn't think twice about shifting forms, destroying everything, and taking you down with it. You cannot fight them."

"And where would you lot be running off to then?"

We all turned to face Rory, ready for her to fill us all in on our destination. She took a slow breath and said, "... We're going to see Uncle Iain."

Her gran spat on the floor. "You can't be serious. He's a fraud."

"He is not. Just because you don't like him doesn't mean he can't help us."

"Look, I respect that you've both got opinions, and this is clearly a family thing. But we don't have time to sit and argue," I interjected. "What we've come here to do needs to be done now. The longer we wait, the better chance there is we lose more than just the object we're after."

"You do what you have to, but I'm not going anywhere." Rory's Gran gestured behind her. "Don't think I'm not prepared for magical nonsense."

We packed up the papers strewn on the table and started for the front door. I stopped just shy of the threshold and closed my eyes, feeling the magic in the world. It ebbed and flowed around me, brushing against my skin like a breeze. I tried to reach for it, but it slipped out of my metaphorical grasp. I briefly recalled Jules telling me that doing magic got harder in the winter for some of us. It must have still been the case.

"What's the matter?" Gethin asked, nudging my shoulder.

"Nothing, I was just trying to give them a little added protection."

"Good idea."

Protecting the place with my own power was all well and good, but it would be stronger if magic bolstering the defenses came from someone who the place inherently trusted.

"Rory, I need you a minute."

The younger woman eyed me nervously as she stepped back to the doorway. "What's wrong?"

"Nothing. I just want to give your gran a little extra protection, even if she doesn't ask for it."

"How?"

"Protection spell. It should be fairly simple, but I thought since this is your home, too, it might be stronger coming from you as well."

Besides, I knew what it had felt like to work with Emerys and Jules' magic in tandem. Part of me wanted to know if I could count on Rory in the same way. And I also couldn't deny my magic craved that new type of connection. If she had foreseen us meeting and working together, it had to mean our relationship was meant for more than just solving this one problem together.

"I'll do anything I can to keep her safe."

I took Rory's hands in mine and gave them a firm squeeze. "Just close your eyes and picture this place covered in a big old bubble of magic. Let it flow out of you."

I watched as she did as instructed. The moment I followed suit, that resistance I'd noticed a moment ago was gone. The world's power pressed against my skin like an impatient pet in need of attention. The magic wanted to help keep this place safe. I put the intent out into the world: *Keep this place and all of its inhabitants safe from harm.*

Lime tickled my nose and coated my tongue as power poured out of me. I could feel Rory's magic feeding into my own. I couldn't quite sense what scent her power gave off, but that had never been one of my skills.

"I think it's pretty impenetrable now," Taron noted, breaking my concentration.

Opening my eyes, I saw a latticework of power gleaming in the sunlight off every inch of the building. I reached out and pressed a hand to it. A shimmer rippled outward from where my palm touched the magical barrier. *Bloody brilliant.*

I turned toward Rory. "So, let's go meet this uncle of yours."

Rory's cheeks were flushed from the exertion of the spell, but she rallied and gestured toward the road. "We can walk to the university."

"He's a professor?"

She nodded. "Come on, I'll fill you in on the way."

We'd made it halfway across the university

grounds before she actually explained that her Uncle Iain taught a mundane subject that made my head ache just thinking about it.

"And why do you think he can help us?" I asked as we passed through a set double doors at the front of a building and down a short corridor.

"Because collecting old books on all kinds of subjects is a hobby of his. If there's going to be anyone around here who can help us figure out how to find this shield, it's him. Besides, he's helped other people before with weird magical problems. And I can always lay it on thick as he owes me for being his niece."

"Anything else we should know about him?" Gethin asked as we reached a closed classroom door.

Before Rory could respond, the door flew open from the inside and a tall man with a beard appeared. He wasn't what I would call classically handsome, but something about him was decidedly alluring. Not in the same way that Taron exuded attractiveness, but I couldn't pull my gaze away.

"Uncle Iain!" Rory exclaimed, throwing her arms around him.

The man—presumably Iain—staggered back under the weight of his niece launching herself onto him in a full bear hug. "This is a surprise. And you've brought friends, Ror."

"Not to be pushy, as we've just met, but mind if we come in? We have a bit of a deadline," I said, stepping into the room without letting him answer me.

The room turned out not to be a classroom, but was instead a small office. Books sat pristine and orderly on the shelves along one wall. I didn't need to get close to tell that some were genuine leather with slightly depressed text printed on the spines. I pivoted back to the man and again found myself staring at him. Out of the corner of my eyes I spotted both Gethin and Taron glowering at him, as if he were the most offensive thing they'd ever seen in their lives. I couldn't help but notice something was off. The bracelet around my wrist warmed against my skin. Apparently, Excalibur agreed. The whole situation felt almost familiar somehow.

"You sure he's actually your uncle?" I addressed Rory.

She extricated herself from the man's embrace and turned to look at me in confusion. "Of course he is. Why would you say that?"

"Weird vibe. Like he's hiding something."

Iain's cheeks burned bright pink as I turned my

critical gaze back to him. The air around us shifted and it was almost as if the light in the room dimmed just a bit. I blinked and when my vision cleared, Iain still stood there, looking a bit greyer around the temples and in his beard.

"You promised," Rory snapped, smacking the man hard on the arm. "You gave your word you'd stop."

"It's a habit, lass. I'm sorry."

Gethin shook his head as if to clear mental cobwebs. "What's going on?"

Rory glared at her uncle and made a sweeping hand gesture, as if to invite him to educate the rest of us on what she meant when she'd said he'd promised not to do ... whatever it was. For his part, Iain remained abashed, keeping his distance. He rubbed the beard on his chin and sunk into the large chair behind the desk.

"I may from time to time use a bit of a glamour."

"Part of why Gran hates him," Rory offered.

"I'm sure that's not really it," he said, still not meeting her gaze. He cleared his throat. "Rory is right, I did make a promise not to do it anymore. But it's so second nature, sometimes I forget I'm doing it."

"Who'd you promise? An ex-lover?" I snorted.

"Someone far more formidable." After a moment he added, "You remind me a bit of her actually. Same sort of feisty energy and desire, to have whatever it was you came for."

For a fleeting moment a familiar scent washed over the room, and I could swear I saw the phantom outline of a particular redhead berating the man who sat across from me. It couldn't be that simple, could it? Did Ezri's legacy reach this far from her home city?

"You're talking about Ezri," I finally offered quietly.

Iain sat up in his seat and gaped at me. "How ..."

"Long story. Short version we're related a ways back down our bloodlines and it seems even from the grave she's trying to help me out."

"Remarkable. I knew she was powerful; I suppose it makes sense a bloodline like that wouldn't just produce one hero."

"Your niece claims you deal with old texts," Taron joined the conversation.

"I'm a collector, yes. I like to track the region's magical history."

"We are in need of anything you have on a certain object."

"You'll need to be more specific."

Rory pulled out the drawings she'd made of the shield and laid them on his desk. "I've been seeing it in my dreams. And Morgan saw it, too, before she came here."

"Came? From where?"

"Camelot," I answered bluntly.

Iain's jaw worked as he tried to process my statement. After a moment of silence, he turned back to his niece's sketches. He traced the lines around the edges. "It looks old, that much I can say for certain. But I'll need some time to dig into what I've got."

"We don't have a lot of time. A man has broken out of federal custody in the United States and is on his way here. He and his mates are after it, too." I pulled out the chair on the opposite side of the desk and sat down. "I don't know if whatever you dealt with for Ezri was life or death, but a little girl is depending on us."

Iain cleared his throat. "Do you have anything more about this shield, a timeframe it might have been created? Something beyond the pencil sketches?"

The compass tucked beneath my shirt turned warm and I tugged it free. I'd forgotten that back in Camelot it had taken on the shape of the shield with its small band of green at its center. I undid the clasp at my neck and laid the compass down on the desk between us. We all stared at the circular metal for a moment in anticipation until it started shaking of its own accord. The object sparked, growing a vibrant shade of green before it reformed into the shape of the shield that Rory had drawn.

"May I?" Iain gestured to the shield on the chain.

"As far as I know it doesn't bite."

I heard Gethin snicker behind me as Iain picked it up, turning it over in his hand, studying the shape of it, and running his thumb over the scored metal. This might be a magical replica, but even I could tell the real thing had seen some action. He laid it back down after a moment and snapped a photo, zooming in on his phone, so the object filled the screen.

"I'm still going to need a little time."

"That's the one thing we don't have," I reminded him.

"Yes, you already said that. Any sense of when this thing was made?"

I shook my head. "Could have been in the last decade or it could have been hundreds of years ago."

"You said the girl from your dream claimed to have forged it." Taron moved a step or two closer to me. "And from your description, she was very young."

"Well, we haven't had that sort of child labor in a long while," Iain muttered.

"And she's currently locked in a dragon's lair in another realm," Gethin added.

I took the compass back and secured it around my neck again. It shifted back into its normal shape as I watched Iain. He jotted down furious notes in some shorthand I had no hope of deciphering. I wished there'd been more information to go on from Laoise. She had looked so frightened in that cave, all alone.

"What do you suppose was in the middle there?" Iain turned his phone to show me the center of the compass' shield model.

"My guess is some sort of stone. Emerald maybe?" I wasn't good with gems.

"That helps." He tapped his chin with the back end of his pen in thought for a moment. I could see his lips moving ever so slightly, as if he were muttering to himself. His gaze was fixed on the bookshelf across the room. Was he making a mental list of possible titles to search through? And if he was indeed going to search through a bunch of old books, did we really have time for all of that?

"Give me an hour."

I wanted to remind him that we were up against a clock, but if I pushed him there was a chance he wouldn't help us, even for his niece.

"Fine. One hour. I just hope you can actually find something in one of your books."

My phone buzzed with an incoming call from Julayne's number, cutting off the conversation. My heart thumped in my throat as I stood and took the call.

"Please tell me you've got her."

"Morgan, she's not here."

Blood rushed to my ears and my vision greyed out. I must have heard her wrong, because there was no way that little girl had managed to get out of the cave on her own.

"What do you mean?" My words sounded miles off.

"No one is here. If there was a little girl being held here, she's long gone."

THIRTEEN

The phone slid from my fingers, clattering to the ground as I stood in Professor Nobles' office. Jules' words rushed through my mind on repeat. *"No one is here. If there was a little girl being held here, she's long gone."*

My vision started to tunnel, blocking out my surroundings and I was only peripherally aware of someone's hand on my shoulder. My legs moved almost of their own accord as that same someone guided me to an empty chair. I blinked a time or two and found myself staring at Gethin, concern etched into the harsh lines around his mouth and eyebrows.

"What happened?" His question was gentle.

"She said no one was there."

"Jules said that?"

I nodded. "Could he have known I'd talked to her and somehow moved her?"

"I know you are concerned with the girl's well-being, as you should be, but even with his long life, I doubt Vilmar is in any state to be giving orders from this realm," Taron offered.

"But it isn't impossible. We don't know how his operation works." Gethin turned to face Taron. "I get that you idolized him, but he's not the doddering old historian you thought him to be. He's the architect of a dangerous secret organization."

"I do not need you reminding me of my own failings." There was a bite to Taron's words I'd never heard before.

"Not to throw myself into the middle of this, but if you want my help, you're going to need to take this squabble elsewhere. I need quiet if I'm going to work," Professor Nobles said, clapping his hands together to draw our focus.

"Come on, we'd better leave him," Rory urged, offering me her hand.

I allowed her to pull me to my feet and trailed her out of the office and back onto the winding paths of the university grounds. I glanced over my shoulder to ensure Taron and Gethin were behind us before I let out a long sigh.

"I feel like I've just been off balance this entire time," I admitted.

"It sounds like you haven't had a minute to breathe. And it also sounds like your mates haven't had time to process their own trauma."

I glanced over my shoulder again to see Taron and Gethin keeping their distance from one another. It wasn't lost on me that the pair kept shooting each other glares as we passed by clumps of students sitting on benches—books in their laps and scarves wrapped loosely around their necks.

"I'm also starting to realize just how much I don't know about what it means to be royalty. What it means to be part of their world. I like to think I was meant for this since that's what I was told my entire life, even if I didn't believe it. But they've lived it for decades and it feels like I'm just pretending."

"I'm sure they don't feel that way," Rory said.

I shrugged. "I mean, Gethin and I sort of had a moment a few months back."

"And you've definitely got something with Hot Dragon Prince."

"Trust me, there's no love triangle happening

here. Gethin is more like a brother to me, and he knows that."

"And Taron?"

"Well, there's been an attraction since we met. But it feels like we keep missing the moment."

Rory gave me a mischievous smirk. "That, I can help with."

She fell back a few paces and looped her arm through Gethin's tense one. "There's this little bakery off grounds that you're going to love." When he shot me an anxious look, I waved him off and Rory gave his arm a tug. "I'm going to need to ply Gran with something sweet to make up for coming to visit Uncle Iain. You can help me pick something out."

I stopped walking, letting the pair of them get ahead of me as Taron moved to stand beside me. He kept his hands tucked in his trousers' pockets and when I pivoted, he wouldn't meet my gaze.

"I'm sorry," I blurted.

"You have nothing to apologize for."

"I dragged you into this mess and now I can't help feeling like I've ruined your passion."

"I am a man of many interests. You haven't done a thing to dampen any of them."

"You don't have to be so chivalrous all the bloody time, you know?"

"Is that what you think I am doing? Giving you false politeness?" That edge returned to his tone.

"No. You've just been so patient, more than any man I've ever met, and I don't know ... it feels strange sometimes. Like you're afraid to upset me." I blew out my breath. "Which I know sounds ridiculously self-centered."

"This may have been the world in which you were raised, Morgan, but I suspect we both feel out of place right now. Off kilter."

I nodded. "Where's a bloody lake when you need it?"

The sharpness of his features melted into a flirty smile. "I am certain we could find something." After a beat, he reached out a hand and brushed his fingertips against my cheek. "Perhaps I am feeling so off, because I couldn't live if something were to happen to you. I have felt this desire to be your shield for some time now."

"I don't quite understand why I'm so drawn to you." I inched closer to him. "The moment I saw you, I couldn't stop thinking about you."

"Well, our first meeting was quite spectacular."

My heart beat a little faster as the image of him

naked, stepping out of the water came to mind. "Is it a dragon thing?"

"I have wondered whether you wove a spell of your own over me." His breath tickled my face as the distance between us diminished further.

There was nothing stopping us now. No dying friends. No exhaustion. For a fleeting moment, my mother's warning about him came into my mind. I batted it away. She didn't get to tell me who I could involve myself with. I dug my fingers into the front of his shirt and made the last centimeters of distance vanish as I pressed my lips to his.

His fingers wound into the hair at the nape of my neck. His entire body was a few degrees warmer than the average person and yet I relished that feeling against my body. In this moment, everything was as it should have been. Time stopped around us as I did my best to memorize every part of him and the way he felt against my skin.

He pulled away first, much to my annoyance, and looked at me through heavily lidded eyes. Any trace of frustration or anger he'd been harboring about the situation appeared to have vanished the moment our lips touched. Nice to know I had that sort of effect on him. I filed that away for later use.

"Well, that was unexpected."

"I'm full of surprises."

"As I am learning every day." He leaned in again and kissed me.

I could have stood on this path in the heart of the university grounds kissing him until the sun burned out. If only the universe had seen fit to give me that little bit of peace. Instead, the little hairs on the backs of my arms bristled against the insides of my shirt sleeves and not even the heat from Taron's body could beat back the chill that settled over me.

I turned slowly to look over my right shoulder. Amongst the scattered groups of students stood an eerily familiar face. My stomach dropped and I found myself immobilized by the sneer on the man's face. It was the younger man who'd accompanied Vilmar through the barrier. He regarded me with curiosity for a moment longer before he held up one hand, giving me a creepy wave, each finger elongated as he did so until they ended in sharp, gut-wrenching talons.

"They're here," I rasped, forcing my body to pivot, so I could face the figure across the path.

"Gethin and Rory," Taron said, concern coloring his words.

There was no time to make sure our friends were unharmed. If we didn't act now, this entire university could find itself in ruin and ashes in minutes. Or strangled to death by that damn mist the Syndicate seemed so fond of generating. As I took stock of our surroundings, I realized no one but the pair of us had taken notice of the man across the quad.

"How likely is it we can convince him to just come in quietly?"

"You're a witch, Morgan. They see anyone not born of dragon lineage as lesser than them. They might borrow and coopt bits of magic they find useful from other cultures ... But make no mistake, to them, dragons are the superior beings."

"If he's here, Vilmar can't be far off."

"Or he's already with sympathizers on this side of the barrier. Your connection noted they had lost the one you fought."

"Only one way to find out."

Before I could think better of it—or let Taron talk me out of it—I closed the distance between myself and the other dragon. He still stood with one hand raised in a malicious mock greeting.

"Right, I think we both know even you aren't stupid enough to shift here in broad daylight, especially cut off from your magic like this," I called.

"You know so very little of my kind," he scoffed as his gaze flickered to a spot behind me. "You barely deserve the title bestowed on you. But my Master likes you, so I will not dishonor him."

"Has history taught you nothing? Purity only leads to loss," Taron called and I picked up on the steady beat of his footsteps as he came to stand shoulder to shoulder with me. "Without differences, without change, we die out."

"We are dragons." His words carried with it the unspoken bias that they were above death.

As I processed his words, his body shifted shape, contorting in a much less languid fashion as skin popped open to reveal the scales beneath. Jagged points erupted around his cheeks and his lips stretched to accommodate a mouthful of teeth. His ears receded into his skull until they were small slits in the scaly surface. Immense wings sprouted from his shoulder joints and I couldn't help but take a step back as he rose up on his hind legs, acrid puffs of smoke curling from his nostrils.

Well, that got people's attention. At least we knew the students weren't under some kind of spell to make them oblivious to the magic around them. Bags and notebooks sat abandoned as people scrambled to get away from the giant fire-breathing monster loping toward them. I had little doubt Excalibur could withstand a few blasts of dragon fire. But would that be enough to hold him off to get the innocents to safety?

"I need you to trust me," I shouted to Taron as I kept my gaze locked on the advancing beast.

"I do not like the sound of that."

"We need to get these people out of here, minimize the damage. They aren't going to understand what I'm about to do, so I need you to make sure they get clear."

"I am not leaving you to face him alone."

"I can handle one little dragon." My tone conveyed far more confidence than I actually felt.

I inhaled, still not looking away from the dragon as it bore down on me. I'd never tried to conjure a portal without looking at where I'd intended to cast the spell. But if I turned my back on this beast, I had no doubt it would turn me into a barbecue, my royal status be damned. Planting my feet, I etched a circle in front of me, but didn't pour any power into it. Not yet. Instead, I jerked my body to the side, sending it behind me. I envisioned the entrance to the university grounds we'd come through earlier.

"Go!"

I didn't wait for him to acknowledge the command. Instead, I focused on the creature as it opened its mouth to shoot flames at me. I raised my hands, envisioning a solid barrier of air to suck all of the oxygen from the flames. My fingers shook as the flames made contact with my spell. My feet skittered back on the pavement, and I gritted my teeth to keep my balance. I wasn't going to let this bastard get the better of me.

The flames petered out as the dragon reached out a hand, talons shining in the sunlight as if to swat me away. I threw myself into a roll to avoid him making contact, scraping up my left arm in the process. Luckily my jacket took the brunt of it. My heart hammered against my ribs as I regained my footing. I could try the spell again that had caught Vilmar at the barrier. It had forced him out of his dragon form and back into mortal flesh and bone. But he was probably expecting something like that.

I glanced around, taking note of the last few stragglers darting for the safety of the portal. Taron was nowhere to be seen. I had to trust that meant he was doing as I'd asked and keeping the civilians safe. As the dragon made another sweeping pass at me, I felt Excalibur warm against my wrist. I recalled the intensity with which Taron had reacted when I'd pulled out the magical blade during our practice session. He'd almost recoiled from it, as if it could have done him serious harm.

Flashing the creature a cocky smile, I pressed a finger to the sapphire at the clasp of the bracelet, summoning the sword into its rightful form and gave it a solid swing at the dragon's incoming forearm. The blade found purchase in between two scales, slicing one clean off. The dragon let out a hideous growl and lashed at me, its tail whipping around at lightning speed.

I wasn't fast enough to avoid the impact and it sent me slamming into a nearby bench, winding me. I coughed as I tried to regain the ability to breathe. The sudden assault was enough to cut off the power to the portal and snapped shut, likely stranding Taron on the other end.

Come on, Morgan. Get up. You can do this.

Pressing one hand to my ribs to check for injury, I staggered to my feet, ready to take another swing at the dragon. In the time it had taken me to regain my bearings, something else caught its attention. I turned to see Taron levitating a good foot off the ground, his eyes glowing bright orange as he slammed a hand into the dragon's spine. If the howl it had elicited from Excalibur's touch was horrible, this was a hundredfold worse. It was as if not just this dragon, but all others like him were crying out. The beast took off into the air, disappearing from view. I made my way across the quad to where Taron stood. "I don't know what you did, but thank you."

"They're vulnerable on their brands that mark them as Syndicate. At least they used to be. Now they know we're aware of them being here."

The compass had provided us with a way to track them, but we hadn't seen them coming. It raised a new question. "How'd they know where we were?"

"That's something I think we ought to consider in a less vulnerable location. Perhaps we ought to retire to the Professor's office."

I returned Excalibur to its less conspicuous form as we hurried off the quad and back to the building where we'd left Professor Nobles. The overwhelming coppery scent of blood hit me the moment we reached the office.

What the hell happened here?

FOURTEEN

The fact I could taste blood on my tongue after suffering no injury suggested just how much carnage lay in the office before me. Fear rooted me to the spot as my mind struggled not to work through worst case scenarios. What if Gethin and Rory had come back early, and the acolyte's compatriots had found them? Or worse, Vilmar had been the one to attack.

Even with the door mostly closed, I could still make out the chaos within the room—papers thrown on the floor and that nauseating smell of blood.

"We need to go inside," Taron urged.

"I don't know that I can," I admitted, taking an

involuntary step backwards, bumping into his torso behind me.

His fingers wrapped tight around my right hand and gave it a squeeze, promising support and solidarity. Whatever lay ahead, we'd face it together. Swallowing the bile rising in my throat, I nudged the door inward with my toe. The hinges whined in protest as the door came up against something heavy blocking it. I squeezed through and found a chair pressed against the doorframe.

Like someone had tried to barricade themself in. I shoved it to one side.

Professor Nobles.

"Professor?" My voice cracked as I called out and got no answer.

I took the moment of uneasy silence to truly survey the room. Books had been thrown across the floor, pages ripped out of several. My heart ached at the fact that so many of what I'd guessed to be first editions had been damaged. I picked my way around the perimeter of the room, finding no sign of the man who'd offered us his help.

"Here!"

Taron crouched behind the desk, and I stumbled over broken books and shredded bits of paper to fall to my knees at his side. Professor Nobles lay on the floor, hand slick with blood as he tried—and failed—to keep more from pouring out of a nasty abdominal wound. The edges were ragged, as if something had dug in its claws and yanked.

"Hang on," I said, tugging off my jacket and wadding it into a ball. I applied it to the wound and replaced the man's hand, doing what I could to apply pressure.

"We need help."

My fingers were now slick with blood, too. With my free hand, I tossed my phone to Taron. "Dial nine-nine-nine. Tell them we need an ambulance at the university."

He didn't miss a beat as he pressed his finger to the screen, standing as he did so. I watched him begin to pace as he waited for the line to connect. I turned my attention back to the Professor.

His skin was ashen and clammy to the touch. He'd been here a while, steadily losing blood. Fuck, Rory was going to lose her shit if she saw this. I pressed the pads of my bloody fingers to his neck, feeling for a pulse. It was faint, but still there.

"Professor, can you hear me?" I leaned in close.

He gave a soft moan and his eyes opened. His lips parted in an effort to speak, but he only succeeded in coughing up blood. Reaching for the sleeve of the jacket pressed into his stomach wound, I did my best to wipe away the blood from his lips.

"Help is on the way. You just need to hang on."

"Sh—" he tried again, but more blood stained his mouth.

"Don't try to talk. Just save your strength." I couldn't help but flash to the flat a week ago, another dying man in my arms. I wasn't going to give up on the professor, but it did give me an idea. I'd coaxed memories before, and I could do it again.

"I'm going to try something." I tried to rest his head in my lap as I gathered my strength and focus. The scent of lime bubbled to the surface, coating my skin like juice as I connected with the man on the floor. I did my best not to worry about the fact his own power didn't fight me as a sign he was barely hanging on.

"Uncle Iain!" Rory's voice boomed from the doorway.

She squeezed through and sat down at his side. "What happened?"

"We found him like this. I'm doing what I can, but the wound is pretty bad."

Gethin appeared in the doorway too and immediately crowded into the space, pulling the bloodied jacket away from the wound. He let out a hiss as he poked at the edges of the wound. Iain shuddered in my lap as Gethin continued to assess the injury.

"I'm here," Rory said, tears shining on her cheeks as she stroked the man's hair.

"I'm so sorry, but I don't know if there's anything we can do to help him." I gave Rory a sympathetic look. "We had a run-in with Vilmar's acolyte and I'm starting to think it was a diversion for the Syndicate to go after Iain."

"But how'd they know where we were?" Gethin reapplied pressure to the wound. Although I could pick up on a hazy purple glow around the fabric.

"How sure are you that the magic you used to track them couldn't be doubled back on us?"

"Not as sure as I'd like to be. But why would they attack him?" Gethin shifted his weight. "Not to sound harsh, but I can understand them going after you and Taron. Royalty, the lost heir and all that. But Iain was only tangentially involved."

"Unless they are looking for the shield as well." Taron reappeared in the doorway. "Medical aid is on the way."

I stood and scanned the room. "This place is a mess. It's possible they found something, or they tossed the place when Iain wouldn't help them and left empty-handed."

"Took ... "Iain's voice was raspy, almost like a death rattle.

"Easy, mate." I knelt down again. "I think I've got a way you can help us without straining yourself."

"What are you going to do?" Rory brushed the tears off her cheeks with the back of one hand, trying hard to be brave in the face of the potential loss.

"In the past, I was able to get glimpses of someone else's memory when they were close to death, I'm hoping I can do the same here."

"Do it."

I turned my attention to the man on the floor. "You okay with this?"

He nodded and his entire body shivered, shock taking over and beginning to shut down his bodily functions. I was running out of time. I gripped his less bloody hand between both of mine and willed the magic that had built up in my body seep into his body, warming him a little. Again, his magic gave no resistance as I searched for the memories of the attack.

In a flurry of images, I caught Iain bent over a pair of books. The door crashed open and the man from Boston appeared, hands already shifted into talons. A woman clad in leather stood just behind him. Red-tinged and full of pain, the rest of the images came in such rapid succession I couldn't make them out. Except to understand that Iain had been gutted and the room trashed. If we were lucky, we'd have time to sort through what he'd gone through and unearth whatever the dragons had gotten their talons on.

Iain gave another full-body shudder just as two paramedics appeared behind Taron. I stood up, ready to lie to them when I spotted a tiny insignia I recognized as the magical law enforcement division. For a split second I was surprised to know they had a branch in Ireland. But only for a second.

"Any of you see what happened?" the male medic asked.

"All we know is it was a magical attack," I replied. They didn't need to know about the existence of dragons. People in this world could believe in a lot, but we didn't need to introduce that particular hiccup.

"Looks like something took a big chunk out of him," the other medic noted as she pulled the crimson-soaked jacket away from his torso.

"Please, you've got to help him," Rory begged. After a ragged breath she added, "He's my uncle."

"Can't make any promises," the medic said, fixing Rory with a sympathetic look. "But we'll do everything we can."

I backed out of the space between the desk and the wall where Iain lay and grabbed Rory by the elbow, guiding her from the area, too. Gethin stood and moved to allow the first medic access to the patient. I turned Rory, so she was facing away from the scene on the floor.

"I know exactly what you're feeling right now." I gripped both of her hands tight to keep her attention on me. "You're angry, hurting, and feel powerless. I've been there. And I know you're going to want to go with him, but I need you. We need you."

"He doesn't have anyone else."

"I know. And that's unfair. But he'd want you here, solving this."

"If I hadn't suggested we come ..." she began.

"No. Don't blame yourself. This was the path we had to take," Gethin piped up.

Taron nodded. "And as horrible and heartbreaking as it is, Morgan's right. This is where we are all meant to be right now."

Behind us, the medics packed gauze pads into the gaping wound and hooked him up to portable monitors. However, it was too quiet as they loaded him onto a gurney and rolled him out of the room. The scent of blood was still heavy in the air, turning my stomach sour.

"We need to figure out what Iain was working on. Grab anything that he might have been looking through. We'll piece together what we can back at the B&B." My voice carried a note of command I hadn't expected.

Without argument, my companions began gathering up the torn papers and books strewn about the room. Rory's shoulders hunched as she straightened some books on one of the middle shelves. As Taron handed her a few more to add to her collection, Gethin bumped me with his shoulder.

"I could sense a bit of that same magic that was in the mist."

I appreciated why he saw the need to share that detail in a hushed tone. "Then we definitely need to keep her focused here with us. Maybe we can get this all sorted before she gets the news."

"If he's got that long."

"We need to be positive. She's going to need that from us."

"We might want to leave before other authorities arrive and detain us," Taron said.

I focused on the empty space in front of me for a

moment before I traced a circle midair. I pictured the front entryway of the B&B in my mind, and it popped into view within the confines of the portal. "Let's go."

One by one, we passed through. As the magic blipped out of existence behind me, I expected Rory's gran to be waiting for us, shot gun in hand to defend her home. Except the area was empty.

"You did tell her to leave," Gethin said, almost reading my mind.

"Didn't think she'd actually believe me and do it. Which is why Rory and I cast protection spell on this place."

"What the hell happened to you lot?" Gran's voice came from the landing behind us.

Rory, who until that moment had kept it together, dropped the books and papers she'd been carrying and bolted up the stairs, throwing herself at the older woman. Without question, her gran wrapped her in a tight embrace.

"Uncle Iain was attacked. It's bad."

"He's with medics and they're doing everything they can," I added. " But we were ambushed by those same crazy blokes who came looking for shelter here."

"There's one standing across the road. Been there since you left."

Taron moved to peer out the window of the front door. "I don't recognize him."

"We knew the Syndicate's network spread throughout this world, too. For all we know, Vilmar showed up and activated everyone or something."

"Has he made any moves to come in?" Taron's brow furrowed as he studied the figure across the way.

"No, just keeps standing there like he's made of stone. Strangest thing is other people don't seem to notice him."

"He's probably trying to scare you; cast some sort of spell to keep anyone else from taking notice."

"Well, he'll only be getting in over my dead body," Gran quipped.

"Gran!" Rory's voice pitched up a few notes.

"Sorry, lass. Poor choice of words."

"The magic we cast before we left is still holding, so with any luck, they won't be able to get in at all."

"Make haste, we ought to see what we can figure out from Iain's notes and papers," Gethin said, starting for the back of the B&B, to the little office he and Rory had sequestered themselves in earlier.

"Is there somewhere we could use that's a bit more spacious?"

"It's not pretty, but we've got a sitting room through there." Gran gestured down the stairs and behind her. "It's got a few chairs and a table, and room to move around."

"Good. That should work." I turned to look at Gethin. "I need you to get all the information we gathered from Vilmar's archive. I have a feeling this is somehow connected." I still didn't understand how the dragons had found us at the university. But it was possible they'd had a network of sympathizers keeping tabs on us the moment we came through the barrier. After all, I had wounded their illustrious leader.

Gethin handed me the books he'd taken from Professor Nobles' office and darted up the stairs past Rory and Gran. Regaining her composure, Rory descended the stairs and led the way to the sitting room. I followed close behind with Taron hot on my heels. It was about twice the size of the bedroom I'd been given with a large bay window facing the street. I pulled the curtains closed to hide our plans from prying eyes.

"What makes you believe the Syndicate and its history is connected to the shield?" Taron appeared at my side as I drew the curtains on all of the other windows in the room.

"Why else would Vilmar be holding the person who crafted the shield captive? It has to be able to hurt them somehow. Right now, it's the only thing that makes sense to me and I'm going with it."

"But you said your friends found no evidence of the girl in the cave."

"I can't explain that. I just have this feeling. I need you to trust me."

"From the moment I met you, I knew I could," he said, his hand brushing my left wrist. I expected Excalibur to react to his touch, but it remained cool and dormant. Nice to know my magical sword didn't see My Hot Dragon Prince as a threat.

"We've got everything, now what?" Gethin set the added parchments and books on the table at the center of the room.

"Now we see how much of the professor's memories I was able to get and hope that the answer is in there somewhere."

FIFTEEN

We stood around the table, piled high with books and other bits and bobs from the professor's office. My three companions all turned to me; expectation written on their faces. I'd had some practice projecting my own memories into the world around me for other people to see. But projecting someone else's was a new trick. Still, they were counting on me to make it work.

"Is something supposed to be happening?" Rory shifted her weight from foot to foot.

"It's about to," I answered, shaking out my hands in an attempt to relieve my nerves.

Taking a slow breath, I let my focus turn inward. I conjured the image of myself in the office tapping into the professor's sporadic memories, colored as they were by fear and pain. They stuttered like a film strip that had come loose. I reached out with metaphorical hands to steady and realign the images flashing through my mind.

"Whoa!" Rory exclaimed, her voice was loud in my left ear.

I opened my eyes and found myself standing back in the professor's office. I hadn't realized I'd projected the memory already. But Iain stood in the middle of the table, bent over the same two books I'd caught in the memory before we'd left the campus.

"Can anyone make out the books he' got there?" I took a step forward, but the image faltered the moment I moved. I was going to need to rely on those around me to get the information we needed.

Gethin stepped up and positioned himself beside Iain's right shoulder. He bent low, as if trailing his finger along the actual page of the text. I watched him mouth words under his breath as he stood up. "Looks like this one might be called Ancient Metal Workings of Ireland and the British Isles."

I took a cursory look at the books piled on the table beneath the memory overlay of Nobles in the center of the room. Nothing with that title stood out to me from this angle. "What else can you see?"

Rory flanked Memory Iain on his left and pulled out her phone, snapping a photo of what he was looking at in the second book. "There looks like some folklore on this page." She bent closer. "Wow, this is like eight hundred years ago."

The Syndicate was older than that, but could it be possible that Laoise was that old, too? If that was the case, then how was she still a little girl after all this time? Too many unknowns swirled in my head, distracting me from the information we needed to pull from the memory.

"Can either of you make out the other text he's reading?"

"Not clearly. It's all a bit ... fuzzy," Gethin replied.

That's what I got for pulling a dying man's memory. Part of me wanted to let the spell drop, so we could properly assess what we had with us. But I wasn't confident I could summon the memory a second time. My head was beginning to ache at the base of my skull.

"I'm going to let it play forward." I looked pointedly at Rory. "I'm not sure what's about to happen, so brace yourself."

I heard her take a shaky breath, but she nodded. "I'm ready."

In my mind's eye, I let the memory play on, similar to an old home movie. The images around us changed. Iain was suddenly no longer alone in the space. and the woman in leather, her hands with talons as sharp as knives, she advanced on him. She didn't speak—or if she did, I wasn't able to pull it from Iain's memory— but she gestured to the two texts on the desk. Her companion began rifling through the other books and papers in the office, tossing them everywhere. Iain moved to try and repel the woman, his hand swiping out in a wide arc, and she staggered backward through the doorway. Iain moved to push the chair against the door as a barricade.

Too bad it did nothing to deter the woman or her companion. After a sudden shimmer, the woman rematerialized in front of him. This time, she plunged her hand into his stomach, that same red mist coating her hand as she pulled away. He fell to the ground, pressing his hands futilely to the wound. Intermittent snippets of noise followed as things hit the floor or broke. The sound of tearing and ripping came next and then the world around us grew dim.

I let the spell drop and looked at Rory. "You, okay?"

She shook her head. "No. Not in the slightest. I'm going to find that bitch and make her pay for what she did to Uncle Iain."

"Believe me, revenge can be a powerful motivator. But you can't let it consume you."

"But you said you understood."

"My aunt was murdered by Seelies. Right nasty bastards who nearly killed me, too. Oh, I wanted to make them pay. But then I realized that Nim wouldn't want that darkness to fuel me. She'd want her death to have meaning." I reached over and pressed a hand to Rory's upper arm. "I don't know your uncle, but from how he was with you, I have to believe he'd want the same for you."

"Doesn't' mean I'm not going to send her into the next county if I get the chance."

"Uh, guys, we have a problem," Gethin announced.

He held up the book he'd identified in the memory, but it was very clear that pages had been torn free. Likely the exact ones we needed. "Fucking brilliant."

"I am finding several books on local folklore, but

nothing looks quite right," Taron added, holding up several texts in one hand.

Rory held up her phone. "Might have a work around." She pulled up the photo she'd taken, and I marveled at the quality of the image. I'd have never thought to take a photo of active magic. For one thing, I had no idea how it would react with modern technology.

I could make out snippets of some story about a girl of immense skill with metal and weapons vanishing on the eve of a great battle. It certainly could fit what the young girl I'd encountered in my dream had said. I still didn't know how this helped us get closer to finding the shield or stopping the Syndicate from getting their hands on it.

Rory tapped away at the screen of her phone and after a moment, let out a triumphant yelp. "Thank you, internet search engines. I was able to put this into a search and it gave me the book title." She turned the phone so Taron could see.

He studied the spines of the books he'd found and set all but one aside. "This might be it."

I held my breath as he opened the book to the table of contents. He glanced at Rory's phone which identified the text as coming from chapter seven of the book. His hands moved slowly as he turned the page until he came to the start of chapter seven. One by one, he flipped through the pages until he came to where the section would have been. Like the other book, the pages were ripped out, too. But I could make out indentations in the pages left behind. I ran a finger over the page before turning to Rory. "Give me a pencil."

She disappeared for a moment, reappearing with several options. I took the first one she offered and set the book on the table, pressing the pencil tip to the page. With quick light strokes, I spread a thin layer of lead over the page, revealing the impression of the words left behind:

Protection for those left behind?
Clan war? Aoife connection?
Caves.

"Well, that's unhelpful," I muttered in irritation.

Rory studied the three phrases then looked back to her phone screen. "I've been able to find a digital copy of the folklore book. It describes a young girl who was said to be gifted with great skill in forging metals and weapons. One night, on the eve of a great battle, she was said to have taken her greatest creation and hidden it. Some said it was out of fear that the enemy would see it coming and give away their position. Others think that it was somehow more a blessing."

"Could be Laoise. I thought it said something about her disappearing?"

"Well, it looks as if it were more likely she left to hide the shield and then she vanished completely. No one ever saw her again. Yet the next day, a great battle was waged, but the people she'd left behind suffered no injuries and even though they were a smaller force, they bested the invaders."

"That explains the first note. But what about the others?" Taron pointed to each in turn.

I stared at the scrawled words and a conversation with Emerys came to mind. She'd told me that the point where our two worlds met had once been the seat of a great battle. Her own kin ... my kin, had fought to protect magic and the innocent. Hadn't one of her relatives been called Aoife? But how would Iain have known that?

Where's the Crystal Cave when you need it to converse with dead relatives?

"He must have known about Aoife from his interactions with Ezri," I suggested. "And maybe the shield's been hidden in a cave?"

"But there have to be caves everywhere. We can't

be certain they even meant this land," Taron pointed out.

Well, I knew one way we could put all the speculation to rest. "I need to talk to Laoise."

"Didn't that happen in a dream?" Gethin arched a brow. "Now's not exactly the best time for a nap."

"This whole bloody trip hasn't exactly been convenient for much of anything." I threw a knowing look Taron's way. He offered a small smile in return. "But there's got to be a way that I can connect with her. For all I know we're bound by magic or blood. Maybe that's how I was able to find her the first time."

"I'm going with you."

I wanted to tell Rory that it wasn't necessary, but the look of determination in her eyes told me that denying her was the last thing I wanted to do. She needed a way to channel her anger and hatred.

"Then we better get comfortable."

"I might be able to mix something that could help you on your way," Gethin said. "I need maybe twenty minutes."

"You've got fifteen."

He left the sitting room without a word and Taron followed him a minute later. Rory and I stood amongst her uncle's books and the artifacts we'd taken from Vilmar's cave. "We're going to solve this and stop them."

She gave me a sad look. "You don't have to say that, but thanks. Then again, aren't heroes supposed to be the eternal optimists anyway?"

I laughed. "Trust me, I'm not an optimist. But I can't see a future where the bad guys get their hands on anything we're after. Maybe it's because I spent the first three decades of my life letting their decisions control my life. Well, I'm done. This is my life and my choice, and I choose not to let them win."

"You are definitely not what I imagine when I think of a princess."

"Yeah, I get that a lot."

"What makes you think you might be linked to this girl by blood?"

"Seems every time I come back through the barrier, I'm picking up more relatives. And your uncle seemed to think she might have been connected somehow to Aoife. Well, I can't imagine that was a very common name eight hundred years ago in this area. And Emerys told me that her cousin was called Aoife."

"Who's Emerys?"

I stared at her dumbfounded. Amidst everything

going on, I'd neglected to fill her in on the other people in my small circle of trusted allies. "She found me a few months back, when the Seelies came for my Aunt Nim and I. She brought me back to Camelot. At first, I thought she was just fulfilling some old prophecy or something, but it turns out she's actually my ancestor. Her bloodline runs through me."

"That would make her really, really old."

"She doesn't look a day over thirty-five." Here's hoping I inherited those genes.

"When this is all over, I'm going to have to leave here, aren't I?" Rory sounded both sad and a little excited by the prospect.

"I mean, that's been the case for other people I've encountered. But I'm not going to make you leave the people you love behind. That seems like the wrong message, you know?"

"I think I'm ready to take that step. Gran won't be happy, but I'm not a kid anymore. I can make my own decisions."

"One step at a time."

Before she could respond, Gethin reappeared with two mugs of something that smelled almost like warm apple cider. "You sure you want to do this in here?"

"It's as good a place as any." I took the mug he offered.

"This should put you out within a few minutes. It's designed to wake you up in about ten minutes. So, here's hoping you talk fast."

I raised the mug to Rory, clinked it in toast and said, "Bottom's up."

We downed the cider and I savored the sweetness of the concoction as it coated my throat. A warmth spread through my body as I settled in one of the chairs, my head lolling to one side. For the briefest of moments, I was reminded of the medicine Gethin had given me during the tournament to knock me out and let my body heal. Just like then, I knew I could trust his handiwork and I sunk into the comfortable sensation of falling asleep.

When I opened my eyes, I stood in the same cave where I'd found the girl before. Only this time, Rory stood beside me. She looked around in awe.

"I knew you would return," the child's voice echoed from a dark corner of the room.

"I tried to send people to get you out, but they said you weren't there," I said.

"There will be time for those questions. But now is not that time. I sense you have come to me with more pressing matters."

"We've come to ask where you hid the shield," Rory said. "We know that there are bad people after it and we're trying to stop them. But they're ahead of us."

"I can't just give you the answers. That would not be fair."

"Finding it is a test?" I picked up on the annoyance in Rory's tone.

"The shield was made for a greater purpose. The ones you face believe they understand its true nature. But only the worthy may wield it."

Where had I heard that before?

"Whatever power you imbued into it is meant to protect people, the innocent. You can't let that fall into the wrong hands. That's why you hid it away in a cave."

Laoise smiled at me. "There is great power in the lands where it is secreted. You have felt it's energy before."

Uisneach.

SIXTEEN

Rory looked at me in the dim light of the cave. "That make sense to you?"

"Oddly enough, it does." I tried to picture the area in my mind. I hadn't ever seen any caves. But then again, I'd only ever been focused on the barrier leading to Albion. And in all fairness, almost every time I'd passed through, I was either on my way to or returning from a quest. Often times I was in hot pursuit of or fleeing something trying to kill me. Doesn't give one much time for sightseeing.

"If you are the hero, I believe you are, then you will find what you seek," Laoise continued, emerging from the corner.

"I have so many questions," I said, crouching down to her eye level. "I know this isn't the best time, but I have to know, was the clan you left behind led by a woman called Aoife?"

She tilted her head to the side in thought. "I heard tell of such a woman, but no, I never knew her."

Well, that dispelled one of Iain's suspicions. And it meant I likely didn't have blood ties to the girl. "I've only ever connected like this with someone who shared my bloodline. So, I thought maybe ..."

"Nature finds ways to connect those who need it most. Even reaching beyond what we know to be true, traversing time or how we think nature should work."

"You ended up in Albion after you hid the shield, didn't you? It's how Vilmar and his acolytes found you."

She nodded. "They knew I would be there. Even in the world of my birth, there were tales of monstrous creatures from beyond. I cannot explain how, but as a very young girl I could sense their coming. One night I woke in such fear that I found myself compelled to my father's forge. I worked until the sun rose."

"Sorry, but you're just a kid. I mean, if you're ten that wouldn't surprise me," Rory interjected.

Laoise jutted her chin out in a show of pride. "I was eleven when the beast caught me."

"Is there anything else you can tell us about the shield? We're flying pretty blind here. I mean we have a sense of what it looks like, but anything else?"

"If you are worthy to wield the shield, it will know. That is all I can say."

"We are going to find a way to free you, I promise."

She offered up a sad smile. "I have waited for a very long time. I can wait a little longer."

She stood and reached out a hand, pressing it to my cheek in a tender expression of kindness. I couldn't resist cupping the girl's hand in my own, committing the feel of her skin to memory, so I wouldn't forget what was at stake if we failed. "You are far more special and important than me," I whispered. "You're so young and yet you had the ability to wield such power that creatures from another realm feared you."

"I am a simple witch. I did not ask for such power."

"The ones meant to bear the mantle never do," I replied.

The edges of the cave began to darken, losing

definition. Gethin's concoction was wearing off. We were out of time. I released the girl's hand from mine and watched as she reached out and did the same thing to Rory. She stood on her tip toes and whispered something in Rory's ear that made the other woman blush and wipe a few tears from her eyes.

"Time's up," I announced as the cave shrunk around us, replaced by utter blackness.

Rory gave the captive a small wave before she vanished. I closed my eyes, letting the warmth from the mug of cider fade away from my consciousness. The dream dimmed into the recesses of my mind, like a fond memory I couldn't quite recall. When I opened my eyes again, I found Gethin and Taron standing nearby, each with worry lines tugging at the skin around their mouths.

"That was the longest ten minutes of my life," Gethin proclaimed as soon as I sat up.

"I still can't believe you've done that before. It was so strange," Rory said, rubbing out a crick in her neck.

"I've gotten used to a lot of strange things over the last few months." I looked back to Gethin. "Is our mystery dragon still standing watch outside?"

"They haven't moved."

"No doubt they're waiting for us to make a move."

"We believe we have found out how they knew where to find us," Taron said, looking displeased.

"Please tell me it's something we can counteract."

Gethin held up his forearm to reveal a thin scratch I hadn't noticed before. It looked almost fresh. "In all the chaos I didn't realize anything had gotten me. But one of them must have injured me before they made it through the barrier."

"How does a scratch mean they were tracking us?"

"I was able to extract a bit of scale from the wound." Taron held up something with a pair of sewing tweezers. "I remembered reading something in one of Vilmar's old texts about how the Syndicate used to track their adversaries. Given enough time, the wound would have healed around the scale, giving them a permanent manner to track Gethin."

"And by extension, you," Gethin added. "But Taron thinks he neutralized it."

"Are you sure?"

"I could feel the power radiating from it when I removed the scale. I exposed it to a bit of my own magic and the radiation ceased."

"He breathed fire on it," Gethin described with a smile. "It was actually kind of fascinating."

"Well, we better test the theory since we know where we're meant to go to find the shield."

"She was able to give you answers."

"Sort of. It lies hidden in a cave at a seat of power. She specifically said I'd been there before. The only place on this side of the barrier I could think of was the barrier itself."

"If they've got members spread out across the region, ones familiar with the convergence of power, they might have already deduced the location, too." Taron laid the scale down on the table.

"Laoise also said that only the worthy can use the shield. She didn't say why the Syndicate specifically was after it. But it sounded like even back eight hundred years ago, they were a threat to this world, too."

"The way she talked about forging it, sounded as if she was almost magically compelled to do it. That suggests there's more to it than just a shield with a pretty gem in it," Rory added.

"Are you going to be able to portal us back?" Gethin eyed me with concern.

I wanted to dismiss his worries. But I'd been throwing around a lot of magic and I'd literally fought a fucking dragon only a couple hours ago. And while the little nap had been nice, it was far from restful. If I had my way, I'd sleep for a week before heading out to face off against the Syndicate. Though at best, I had time to grab a sandwich on the go.

"I'll manage. Though I could use a little of your culinary skills before we head out. And we need to fill in Gran on what's happening. She needs to know what Rory's walking into."

As if on cue, Rory's gran walked into the room. "Just had a call from the hospital."

Rory blanched as she waited for her gran to speak. I stood and moved to give the girl's hand a supportive squeeze.

"Apparently, I was listed as his next of kin. He's been in surgery since he got there. They said it was touch and go for a while, but he's stable now."

"Oh, thank God," Rory said. If she hadn't already been sitting down, I'd have expected her legs to give out on her.

"That's great news," I said. "He's a fighter."

"I know he's not out of the woods and he lost a lot of blood, but I think I needed to hear this before we left," Rory said.

I couldn't help but picture Laoise whispering in

her ear. Had it been to reassure her that her uncle would make it? Or was it something to do with the shield?

"Where are you lot going now?" Gran asked.

"It's probably safer if you don't know the specifics. But we're hoping the bloke across the way will follow us when we leave," I explained.

"Let me gather some things to take with us. If you're planning what I think you are, then we're going to have a little time to eat before you need to portal," Gethin said.

"Brilliant."

I left Rory's side and made my way back around to the front of the B&B, heading up to the bedroom I'd used the day before. I gathered my belongings, and stepped into the room Taron and Gethin shared and grabbed their bags, too. By the time I made it back to the sitting room, Gethin had already put together several packs of sandwiches and sliced fruit. Taron had assembled the documents and arti-facts from Vilmar's archive into the original bag Gethin had brought it in.

"You aren't coming home again, are you lass?" Gran stood beside Rory, looking at her with more affection than I'd seen in the older woman's body language since meeting her.

"Not for a while, Gran. At least, I don't think so anyway."

"You weren't meant to putter around this old place with me for the rest of your life. So, it's good you're getting out, seeing the world."

I studied Rory's expression. She was clear-eyed and looked confident. Perhaps knowing her uncle was still alive would be enough to keep her going. I opened the curtains of the front-facing window and spotted the bloke across the way. He still just stood there like a sentinel. I shouldered my bag and took one of the packs of food Gethin offered.

"I have to say, I'm kind of surprised Iain's hanging on." He was careful not to speak loud enough for Rory to hear.

"Maybe the exposure was small enough that his body, once it wasn't fighting to keep the blood inside, could fight the poison off. Like an infection."

"Morgan, I want to apologize," he started, but I shushed him with my hand.

"Don't you dare apologize. None of us had any idea what they'd done. It isn't on you. All we can do now is focus on what's ahead. There's no point in looking back at what might have happened."

"Right. I just can't help feeling like I've been holding you back a lot lately."

"Sod off. You have been amazing, Gethin. I wouldn't be where I am without you."

He glanced back at Taron. "He wouldn't agree."

"To be fair, some of that is thinking with a different head."

Gethin made a strangled gulping sound and adjusted his glasses. "Did not need that image thank you very much."

I chuckled. "Oh, I don't know. It's a pretty nice view."

"Stop. Please stop. Or just put me back in the cave of death mist. I think I'd prefer that."

We both devolved into a fit of laughter, the tension melting out of his features. I clapped him on the shoulder as we stood side by side and I was reminded why I liked him so much. He truly felt like a younger brother; someone who I could joke with, but who always had my back.

"Right, we better get going," I said, regaining my composure. "We're going to head for the university on foot. Just to see if that bloke decides to follow us. And once we're sure he's on our trail, we'll get to the barrier, find the shield, and kick some evil dragon arse."

"And if they are still tracking us?" Rory accepted one of the other food packs Gethin was holding.

"Then we'll have a nasty welcome party when we get there."

"Guess we better be prepared for anything then."

Taking a deep breath, I led the way out of the sitting room, and back around to the front door of the B&B. I could still feel the spell Rory and I had cast on the place and its occupants. I didn't know how long it would stay intact, but I had seen Rory's gran defend her home from unwanted strangers. The older woman had resorted to mundane means of protecting herself, but I'd seen her family's magic in action. She wouldn't go down without a fight.

Stepping back onto the street, I locked eyes with the dragon across the way. I gave him a smirk before turning and heading up the road. My companions fell into step around me. I led the pack at a meandering pace, even though my body wanted to be going at an all-out sprint.

"He's flanking us," Taron said in a low tone as he fell into step beside me.

"But he's not making any sudden moves," I noted.

"He only seems to be keeping pace."

"What if I duck off one way for a couple of streets?" Gethin suggested. "If he keeps following you, then maybe that means he assumes someone else will track me?"

"Worth a shot." I gestured to Rory. "Go with him. Meet back up in two blocks."

At the next cross street, Gethin and Rory peeled off, taking a right turn away from us. Taron and I continued on the route forward. I glanced over my left shoulder after we'd gone half a street. The bloke was still tailing us. But he had something in his hand. It could have been a walkie talkie or a phone.

"He might be calling in reinforcements," I said.

"I think you may be correct."

Which suggested he didn't have a way to track Gethin anymore. I ducked into the first shop I spotted on our side of the road and pulled out my phone, dialing Gethin's number. It only rang once before he answered. "Looks like your trick worked. We're coming to you."

"Okay. We're at the next intersection."

I hung up and wound my way through the small boutique selling retro clothes until I found someone behind the counter. "Hi there, this is going to sound a bit strange, but do you have a back exit?"

The clerk glanced at the pair of us. "What for?"

"I think my ex has been following us. I keep

seeing him across the road ... and it was a bad break up," I lied.

She seemed to buy my story, because she gestured to a space behind a wall of clothes. 'Through there. Takes you out to the street one over."

"You are a life saver," I said and pushed through the clothes hangers.

Moments later, we spotted Gethin and Rory at the corner. I gestured for them to make their way back to us. This was a secluded enough place to create a portal.

Time to find that shield.

SEVENTEEN

I could hear a commotion from within the shop. Clearly our tail had realized where we'd gone. Momentarily, my heart skipped a beat as I pictured the unsuspecting shop clerk facing off with a very cross dragon. I hadn't meant to put her in harm's way.

"We need to go," Taron urged.

I opened the pack of food Gethin had given me, scarfing down half the sandwich and orange slices as quickly as I could. I didn't question why all of a sudden, I felt a burst of adrenaline and energy course through me. Instead, I latched onto the rejuvenated feeling and let it fuel the spell already forming in my mind. I pictured the semi-secluded area of grass just behind where the public gathered. Tracing a circle in midair, I opened the portal and my companions darted through without question.

I was about to step through when I heard something crash behind me. The door opened and the clerk ran out looking disheveled with a bruise forming over her right eye. We locked gazes, she registered the portal a moment before I opened my mouth to speak.

"He's coming," she shouted. She gave me a knowing nod and gestured toward the portal, as if she understood I needed to go through it. I guess mundanes knowing about magic wasn't just a London or a Boston thing.

"Thank you."

"Go!"

I ducked through the portal, closing it as fast as I could, hoping the clerk had time to lead the dragon away before he caught sight of where I'd gone. . It winked out of existence just as I heard the clerk shout something undiscernible, antagonizing the bastard. Brave girl. I turned to see the area around us teaming with tourists. How they hadn't spotted us was a mystery for another day. The sky overhead was starting to darken towards evening. They would be leaving soon. For now, we could blend in with the crowds; maybe use the still active staff to our advantage.

"I've got an idea," I said and led our quartet toward a young man wearing what looked to be a tour guide uniform holding a large umbrella over-head. I could see the text 'Group 7' printed on the exterior of the umbrella.

"Excuse me."

He turned, umbrella still held aloft as if he was more comfortable in that position than any other. "Yes?"

"We were hoping you might be able to help us. My friend's uncle told us about this old bit of folk-lore, and we wanted to see if it was true."

"Lots of stories about this place. You'll have to be a bit more specific, love."

"Well, he said there was some super rare shield secreted away in a cave nearby. He couldn't remember the exact location. But he's in the hospital right now and we'd love to cheer him up by showing him we found it."

Lies were always easier when seeded with a nugget of truth.

"Not many people know about that. The story goes that a little girl forged a shield on the eve of war with a neighboring clan. She hid it in the hills surrounding this region and gave her life as a way to protect her people."

"You wouldn't happen to have an idea where those hills might be?" Gethin stepped up, producing a map from his pack.

Where the hell did he get that?

The tour guide reluctantly set down his umbrella and accepted the map from Gethin. He unfolded it, tracing the areas marked out as terrain on the map. "While I can't say for certain, I know some historians have searched in this region. It's about half an hour's walk. But you'll want to hurry. We close in ninety minutes, and you can't be here after we close."

"We'll be gone before then, promise." I batted my lashes at him and pressed my fingers to the top of his hand as I took the map back. I caught Taron glaring at the man so intensely I thought the tour guide might combust. "You've been a huge help."

"My uncle is going to be so thrilled," Rory added with a wide grin.

"Happy to help."

I started walking in the direction the tour guide had pointed us. I glanced back, waiting for him to resume his umbrella holding and then headed the opposite way. I could sense at least Gethin wanted to ask what I was doing, but I held up a hand until we were well out of earshot and sight of the guide, and not to mention any other potential prying eyes.

"He said we needed to go that way," Gethin finally blurted, holding up the map.

"He said historians looked there. If someone had actually found the shield, it wouldn't be there anymore. Someone would have recognized it for what it was, and it would be in a museum somewhere or in someone's private magical collection. That means they were off base."

"But from looking at the map, these are the only areas that might have caves nearby," he continued, laying the map flat on a nearby outcropping of rock.

"Exactly. So, that's where we're headed."

"Not to worry anyone, but our friendly tour guide is on his phone and he's looking this way," Rory noted.

I pulled the compass from beneath my shirt. The bit of magic Gethin had worked up to track the Syndicate wasn't active. And it hadn't signaled that the guide was one of their members either. Had their countersurveillance somehow shorted out Gethin's spell? I turned to ask Taron that very question, but he was gone. Panic gripped my chest for a minute before I spotted him bent down, pretending to tie his shoe near the guide. After a moment, the guide stowed his phone and walked toward a small cluster of school-aged students and a collection of bored-looking adults.

Taron rejoined our group a minute later, moving with cheetah-like speed. "He is not Syndicate, but he may be working for them. I couldn't sense any magic from him, so it's possible they bribed him the mundane way."

"With money." I could almost understand the desire. This had to be a thankless job and I doubted it paid well. If someone had asked me to make a call if anyone came asking about the local caves, I'd probably have said yes, too.

But that meant the Syndicate was expecting our arrival, which left us on the back foot yet again. Anger bubbled hot in my gut at how unfair it felt. But nothing in life is ever fair. And everything to this point had been a test of one sort or another. Sure, I assumed that obtaining the shield itself would be its own ordeal, like Excalibur had been. But persevering in the face of adversity was its own kind of test. A good leader had to be able to keep fighting, even when all seemed lost.

"So, they know we're on the way. We knew that might be a possibility."

"If we can find a way to surprise them, throw them off guard, we could regain the upper hand," Taron said.

"How would you suggest we do that?" Gethin folded up the map and stowed it in his pack.

"They have been observing us, at least to some extent. They likely don't perceive you as much of a threat."

"You're going to hold nearly dying over me forever, aren't you?"

"A weaker man would have succumbed in moments. You fought like a true warrior. But you are not a dragon. That means they will always see you as less than them."

"And Vilmar still has some sort of affection for you. He might be more willing to at least talk to you," I said, starting to realize what he was proposing.

"If we can keep their focus, then you can slip in and take what they're after."

"For the record, I dislike being the bait," Gethin grumbled. "But I can see the logic."

"Besides, I have a feeling that we're meant to do this together," Rory added, looping her hand through mine. "Come on, I think I've got an idea."

I didn't like leaving the guys to their own

devices. It felt safer sticking together until we abso-lutely had to split up, especially after the dragon attack on the quad. But Rory only led me a few paces away, holding up her phone in camera mode. It was positioned to show us what was going on behind us. I had to hand it to her, she had picked up on subterfuge quickly.

"That bloke who was watching the B&B gave me a plan," she explained as she continued to scan our surroundings. For now, no one appeared to be paying us any special attention.

"You want to make it, so they won't see us coming?"

"Well, sort of. I mean, we could clearly see him, but people around him couldn't. They just walked by as if he weren't standing there."

"Selective blind spots."

"We need Taron and Gethin to be able to see us, but not all the bad guys. It can't be all that difficult to do."

"I've never tried to do anything like that before. Have you?"

"No, but I mean it can't be that hard."

"Okay, let's give it a go. Try to make the guys see you, but hide yourself from me."

She handed me the phone so I could keep

checking our surroundings as I felt her magic bump up against me. For a moment, she flickered out of view, but. I could still sense a presence next to me. If I were walking around, I might realize there was something in the way. But I wasn't sure if that meant I'd walk around it or not.

"Oi, you two, can you see Rory?" I called.

Both of them turned in unison and Gethin's eyes narrowed. "No."

"She's right there next to you," Taron said, gesturing to the apparent empty space beside me.

Rory let out a huff and reappeared. "I was really trying to make it so only you could see me."

We had to be missing something. We'd all seen the dragon outside the B&B. But all the people going by hadn't. What was different about us and then?

"Rory, do you live in a predominantly mundane area?" Gethin rubbed his chin in thought.

"I guess. I never really thought about it much."

"I would venture it would be simpler to conceal yourself from anyone without magic than to differentiate between types of magic," I said.

"You're trying to camouflage yourselves to hide from our enemies. Clever." Taron's angular features almost glowed with admiration.

"I was trying to make it so you would both be able to see us," Rory replied.

"I should still be able to, even if you only hide yourselves from anyone with dragon-based magic,' Gethin said. "Taron won't be able to see you, but I'll have his back."

"I wish we had more time to figure out what we were walking into," I muttered. "We don't know anything about how these caves are connected, or even if they are. Let alone if there's multiple ways in or out."

"We'll have a little time to see what we can come up with off the internet," Rory took her phone back. "He said it was a half hour walk. So, we'd better get started."

I caught Taron tugging on the hem of his shirt and I reached out to stop him. "I get what you're thinking, but we don't want to draw attention to ourselves. A dragon circling the hills would be a dead giveaway. Besides, I'm guessing since they're all connected by that brand, they'd spot you for an intruder in a heartbeat. You may not be next in line for the thrown anymore, but I am not going to explain to your parents how I took you on one road trip and got you killed by purist lunatics."

"I can be stealthy, stay high enough to be out of

sight of anyone mundane on the ground. We need to know what we're walking into." He stroked my cheek. "I am afraid my own stubbornness is going to win out here, Morgan. I appreciate your desire to protect those in your company, but I can handle myself."

"You go and you come straight back. Don't be a hero."

He offered me a deep bow that from anyone else would have been mockery. With him, it was earnest and that made it all the more infuriating. He slipped away out of sight to make the transformation and a few minutes later, I caught sight of a large, winged creature rising into the clouds. The sunlight glinted for a split second off bronze scales and my heart skipped a beat.

"I know the rest of them are trying to murder us, but that's pretty bloody cool," Rory pointed out.

"Yeah. Let's get moving."

I followed the trajectory he'd taken and found his clothes piled in the grass. Scooping them up, I stowed them in my bag and let Gethin lead us onward toward the western system of caves. The world around us grew quieter the farther we got from the hustle and bustle of the tourist traps. I breathed in the clean, unpolluted air and felt the world's magic swirl around me.

"You guys feel that right?" Rory's voice was full of awe as we crested a small hill that led down into a lush green valley. I could make out a system of dark mounds ahead of us that could very well have been caves.

"This place is untouched by a lot of modern life. Magic is raw here, more palpable," I replied. "I think that's partly why the barrier exists here. The world's magic is so strong it couldn't help but connect beyond what we can see."

"It's kind of overwhelming."

"We're going to need to use it to our advantage."

"How?"

"You were born in this world, which makes you more directly tied to it. And I spent much of my life here, I think it somehow recognizes me. Those blokes don't belong. So, if we can find a way to make the magic around them reject whatever they throw at us, then maybe we can take them out without this turning into a blood bath."

I shouldn't have said a damn word. As we approached the system of caves, I sensed a presence coming from behind. I didn't want to turn and face whoever had flanked us, but I knew I didn't have a choice. I pivoted slowly, hoping against hope that Taron had caught up and simply needed his clothes back.

Instead, the woman who'd nearly disemboweled Professor Nobles stood there in a skintight leather get-up that made me think she was auditioning for the part of a discount Dominatrix. Her skin was much paler than Taron's and her hair was almost snow white. Her eyes though, mismatched brown and green were eerie. I hadn't noticed those details when I'd run through the professor's memories. Maybe he'd been so caught off guard by the assault that he hadn't felt it important to commit it to memory.

"You thought yourselves clever, didn't you?" she sneered.

"Well, I mean we made it this far with all the shit you'd thrown our way. Yeah. I do think we're pretty clever."

So, much for going in unnoticed.

EIGHTEEN

I didn't think. Instead, I launched myself at her, letting my forward momentum take us both to the ground. Her hair, done up in a thick plait draped over one shoulder provided an easy hand hold for me to keep her pinned down. It wasn't elegant, but I raised my hand and slammed my free fist into her face. I felt something crack on impact and prayed I hadn't just broken my hand. The lack of searing pain suggested it was the dragon who'd just broken something. From the way her nose gushed blood when I pulled away, it seemed clear that was the case.

She reached up to try stemming the flow of blood and throw punches with her other hand. I didn't let her get in any hits. I pinned her left hand to the ground and slammed my fist into her face again. More blood gushed, coating my skin and turning my stomach. But she was slower to react this time.

She managed to use her hips to buck me off and I rolled sideways, bumping into Rory's legs as she and Gethin stood immobile. In that moment, I almost longed for the tournament uniforms. The material had seemed to repel most bodily fluids, at least for a time. As it was, I wiped my hand on my shirt, staining it rust colored. The dragon staggered to her feet, and I watched her body undulate. It was a move I'd come to recognize meant fire was incoming.

Excalibur practically forced my left hand up to block my face, even as it remained in bracelet form. Given the damage it had done on the last dragon I'd fought, unsheathing the blade seemed a better move. This time the jewelry took the first jets of flame to leave her mouth. Seconds later, I'd shifted the sword into its fighting form and raised the flat of the blade to deflect her attack. In my peripheral vision I caught Gethin drag Rory to the ground as more flames shot out to either side of me.

The dragon's mismatched eyes widened as she registered the sword in my hand. Maybe no one had told her about the mythic blade. Or maybe she hadn't believed a mere witch could wield it. Either way, her moment of indecision in the aftermath of her first attack left her vulnerable. I was about to lift the sword again to advance on her when something heavy struck the back of her head, sending her crumpling like a rag doll to the ground.

Taron stood behind her in all of his naked glory, hefting a stone the size of a large watermelon. He gave me a quick smile before holding out his other hand. "I believe you have something of mine?"

Gethin grabbed Rory by the arm, spinning her away so she wasn't staring at Taron. I pouted at him before digging in my pack for his clothes. He pulled them on and gestured to the caves at the far end of the system. "From what I could see, they've concentrated their efforts over there at the end."

The sky overhead continued to darken and with it, the temperature dropped a good two or three degrees. I shivered without the benefit of my jacket and the sticky dampness of the blood now staining my shirt. If all went well, a chill would be the least of my worries. And we were walking into a situation with literal fire breathing monsters.

"You're sure they didn't see you, right?"

"I stayed high and in cloud cover. I didn't see any airborne scouts and I circled three times."

"You could have warned us about her," Gethin said.

"She happened upon you while I was doing my last sweep. My apologies."

"How did they find the caves?" Rory asked.

"My guess, they figured it out from the books they stole from your uncle," Gethin answered. "And with the guide on the payroll, or at least acting as an informant, it's possible he gave them directions. Well, let's hope she didn't have a chance to let anyone else know we'd made it this far." I looked at Rory. "Our plan can still work." Turning back to Taron, I gestured to the outcropping of rocks ahead. "Was there any indication of a back entrance or any other way in? "

"I couldn't make out anything from within, but I did see a few guards patrolling the other side of the cave system. That would lead me to believe there is another way in."

"Then we take it."

"But he just said there's guards patrolling," Rory noted.

I flexed my hand. "I think we can handle a few guards."

Rory pulled her hair into a knot at the nape of her neck. "I admire your optimism, but I am not a fighter."

Taron made a gesture toward his back. "If you're able to strike them in the center of their brands, it should temporarily paralyze them."

"Today is so weird," Rory murmured.

I took her by the hand. "Okay, time to turn invisible. Remember, you want to keep us hidden from anyone who isn't a witch."

"Now might be a really bad time to ask, what if they're working with evil witches?"

"Trust me, they do not mix with non-dragons unless absolutely necessary. The fact one of their founders came through the barrier and was injured, they wouldn't want anyone of another race near him," Taron said confidently.

I squeezed Rory's hand. "You've got this."

I felt her magic ripple over me as she poured out her intent into the world. It almost felt as if something was tickling my skin as it went. I turned and studied Gethin and Taron's faces. Taron looked mildly surprised to find us missing. Gethin offered a small thumb's up to signal it had worked properly.

Together, Rory and I approached the cave system, making our way around the outside of the outcropping. I glanced back over my shoulder to see Gethin and Taron approaching the main entrance. I said a silent prayer that they'd be safe as they disappeared from view. I paused mid-step, straining to hear any signs of distress, but nothing came.

We continued on, our footsteps echoing on the rocky surface. I should have realized we needed to muffle our approach. But it's too late, the two guards on patrol turned at the sound of our footsteps. I grabbed Rory to keep her from moving forward.

"They wouldn't be so stupid," one of the guards said.

Tapping Rory's shoulder to draw her attention, I mimed levitating in the air with my other hand, then pointed to where the guards stood. I then mimed smacking them between the shoulder blades. She nodded in understanding and my magic built up around me, as if creating unseen, silent steps in the air. We crept around them side by side until we'd reached the spot intended. Their backs were exposed, revealing their brands, identical to the one I'd seen on Vilmar. I could almost feel the magic swirling within it, connecting them together even as it marked them as members of the Syndicate.

I didn't think just smacking them would be enough to subdue them. When Taron had taken out the other dragon, it had appeared to me like he was almost tearing the brand in some way.

'Unmake the bond'

The soft voice I associated with Excalibur echoed in my head. I'd almost forgotten I hadn't returned it to its innocuous form before we made our trip around the caves. I gestured for Rory to take a step back without breaking contact with me. Her hand shifted to hold on to my upper arm. It freed me to turn the blade, so that the sharp edge lined up with the center of the brand on the dragon directly in front of me. Steadying my feet I brought it down hard. The brand shimmered and went dark in an instant.

He didn't have time to cry out before I'd struck down his partner. Their bodies shuddered as they hit the ground. The moment they hit the ground; I could pick up on commotion within the cave. The other Syndicate members inside must have felt the link snap with their allies. Apparently, taking them out this way had betrayed our presence. Well, too late to change it now.

"Don't drop the spell yet," I whispered as I led the way into the cave.

"I think they know we're here," she replied.

"Yeah. It wasn't going to stay a secret for long."

The cave was lit by globes of fire suspended about six feet in the air. They were almost beautiful in the way they shifted from the warm oranges and yellows to the harsher blues and whites of the kind of flame that would consume you in an instant. But they directed us into the heart of the cave where piles of rubble sat scattered across the floor. I could make out the edges of something metallic and worn sticking up from the floor, as if the shield had seen battle before. But that didn't make sense. From everything we'd heard, Laoise had secreted the shield away before anyone could use it and yet it somehow protected her people from attack.

"You owe me an audience, Vilmar. Our history should earn me that much." Taron's voice echoed from beyond the small excavation site.

"You were a necessity in preserving my power," Vilmar responded. "I took no pleasure in our time together."

"See, I don't believe you when you say that. You nurtured my curiosity and hunger for knowledge. You let me in, you shared pieces of your own history without even knowing it." Gravel crunched beneath Taron's feet as he moved farther into the cave. "Were you hoping I might one day join you? That I would forsake my blood, my family and see things your way?"

"Oh, I long ago gave up on that aspiration. I saw the devotion you carried for your blood, for your role as a royal. I could no sooner burn that out of you, as I could cleanse the world of the lesser magics."

"As one of those lesser magics, I've got a bone to pick with you." Gethin's voice rang out in the conversation and it stopped me in my tracks.

No, no. Shut up.

"He speaks? Well, I suppose I have grown complacent in my old age, but I assumed you dead, boy." He drew out the last word, as if that made it more of an insult.

"He is stronger than any of those you would call your acolytes. He is honorable and cares for those around him, no matter their station or their magical origins."

"Also, we're not as easy to kill as you thought. Because that man you sent your acolytes to assault to get here? He's already recovering."

"Lies," Vilmar spat.

"You can check if you want, but he's going to be just fine." I caught Gethin making small shooing motions with his left hand. Taron looked oblivious. The invisibility spell was still working.

I turned my attention back to the partially buried shield. I couldn't understand why they'd stopped the excavation. Surely the arrival of two combatants wasn't enough to distract all of them. As I rounded the rubble, I saw a partially shifted dragon laying prone on the ground. Their torso and upper arms were covered in scales and their face was androgynous enough I couldn't make out it's sex. They looked to be sporting jagged cracks in their armored skin. Each crack oozed a nasty-looking and pungent pus. I guessed that was what happened to the unworthy.

Good to know.

The blade in my hand hummed with power, pulling me forward like a magnet to stand before the partially revealed shield. As the dragon flames over-head shifted their colors, I could see the metal, worn and beaten as if it had been through many battles shimmer, revealing the state it had been in when its creator had first secured it here. At the same time, I sensed a bit of the girl's magic in the air around us.

"What now?" Rory whispered in my ear.

"No bloody clue."

I reached out my other hand and pressed a trembling hand to the exposed metal. I held my breath, waiting for the searing pain and pus to erupt over my own body. Yet, all I felt was warmth, like the magic linking the shield to Laoise's people recognized me and was welcoming me home. I nodded for Rory to touch it and when she did, a look of peace washed over her face.

In a flash of images, I saw the shield as if it had been the day the child had hidden it here. And somehow as battle raged between her people and the invaders, the shield took the brunt of all the strikes, as if someone had literally carried it into battle. And yet, I somehow understood that the shield's magic allowed it to bear the brunt of the violence without having to be present. Over time, those who had called Laoise kin changed, evolving and still whenever conflict raged, the shield bore the weight of it, taking on fresh dings and scrapes. Only the gem at its center remained pristine and untouched.

I blinked as the images receded. I couldn't help but smile at Rory as she opened her eyes again. Her expression of awe mirrored my own. Neither of us pulled away from the object, even as a loud rumbling echoed around us. I looked up in time to see the ceiling beginning to shake. Dust and rock crumbled around us. In a rush of motion, the shield came free.

Maybe it was the sudden change in our surroundings or maybe it had something to do with being in contact with the shield itself, but we were no longer hidden from prying dragon eyes. All faces turned to find Rory and I holding the shield between us.

"I'll be taking that," Vilmar said, extending a clawed hand in our direction.

"Over my dead body," I retorted.

He offered a wicked grin. "Gladly."

NINETEEN

Vilmar might be old as dirt, but he moved fast given the confined space. I barely had time to drag myself, Rory, and the shield to the ground before his taloned fingers were within range of my face. I couldn't explain why, but I didn't want to let the shield go. Part of it was obvious; keep it out of the hands of the ruthless lunatic actively trying to slaughter me. But there was a deeper connection that I couldn't quite put a name to that compelled me not to break contact.

Around us, Vilmar's acolytes turned their attention to Gethin and Taron. I wanted to protect them, but I had to remember they were both capable of defending themselves. They would have each other's backs. Vilmar was my only priority now.

"We need to use what's around us," Rory grunted as she tugged me and the shield back toward the way we'd come in. "Isn't that what you said? Use our connection to the world's power to our advantage."

"Right." I nodded toward my hands, each occupied with an object. "It's like I can't put either of them down."

"Same. Even the thought of letting go makes me want to vomit."

"Maybe we're doing something right then?"

I heard Vilmar let out a bellow and caught sight of something striking him upside the head. I craned my neck far enough to see that Taron had lobbed a chunk of dislodged rock at him in a bid to give us time to escape. As much as I appreciated the gesture, we wouldn't be running away. There was no chance we'd leave our friends behind.

I looked at the blade in my left hand. "I need you to take a back seat, just for a minute. I promise, you'll get your shot."

The blade glowed bright blue, but when I uncurled my fingers from the hilt, I found it sort of hovered beside me. That was new. I pressed my hand against the rock around us and in an instant, I could feel every structural point keeping the ceiling from caving in. With a single thought, I could collapse the cave all around us. The dragons might survive, but it would take them a while to break free. Us on the other hand, even with the connection to the shield, I didn't like our odds. But maybe we didn't need to totally bring the roof down.

"We can stop him in the rubble," Rory said.

"Just what I was thinking."

"When this is all over, you're going to need to explain how I knew that."

"Magic, mate. It can do amazing things."

In unison, we held out our free hands and the rubble that had been cast aside by the excavation effort zipped along the ground, piling around Vilmar's legs until he was held fast. He let out another growl and this time his eyes flashed orange a split second before his body undulated and a stream of flame hurtled toward me.

There wasn't time to get down. On instinct, I held the shield aloft, doing my best to position myself in front of Rory. The shield let out a high-pitched ringing as if someone had struck a very tiny bell as the flame hit it. The world around me grew a little hazy, like I was looking at the space through a blurry window. Through the blur I could just make out Gethin's hands moving in a fluid motion, summoning rock to block one of the oncoming drag- on's attacks. It solidified into a makeshift shield just in time to block the dragon's meaty fist raking through the air at him.

Taking my eyes off my opponent was the wrong move. In the few seconds I found myself distracted by Gethin's magic, Vilmar had freed himself and advanced on Rory and my position. Somehow, he'd also fully shifted his form as he did so. He was much too large for the space available. His wings scraped the ceiling, compromising the structural integrity of the cave, and causing the walls to shake.

"It's about to collapse!" My voice barely regis- tered in my own ears.

Across the cave, I saw Gethin reach overhead, his shoulders shuddering as he literally kept the stone from burying us all alive. He wasn't going to be able to hold that for long. But he wouldn't have to do it alone. Taron emerged from behind him, fully shifted and gleaming in the fire light. He spread his wings and somehow, I knew he'd keep the stone aloft as long as we needed.

"He's getting ready to attack again," Rory called, pulling me to my feet.

"We need a better plan."

"Or any plan," she countered.

"You offering one?"

"Take the shield and run? Let this place cave in?"

"We don't take lives. Not unless we have no other choice," I retorted.

The spot where Rory's hand met the shield's edge grew red and angry. She let out a hiss of pain and I could see a thin vein of flesh starting to separate in the delicate skin between her thumb and forefinger.

"Rory, I know you're angry with them for what they did, but you know we can't stoop to their level. You are better than that. You are so much greater than what they think you are. I can't do this without you. I think we both know that."

Her face settled into a look of determination, and she exhaled slowly. "I'm sorry. I just ... I've lost a lot and sometimes it gets too heavy, and it overtakes me."

"I understand. Truly. But you are worthy of this shield. You want to protect the people you love. That's got to be stronger than your need to make them feel the same pain they inflicted on you."

She nodded and the skin closed up, returning to her normal complexion. Vilmar's hulking form bore down on us, and his talons knocked me off balance, dislodging the shield from my hand. As I slammed into the rock, I felt the sense of peace disappear. Air fled my lungs as I made contact with the rough surface behind me, and Excalibur clattered to the ground a few feet away.

If a dragon could laugh in shifted form, I'd say that was exactly what Vilmar did as he took a couple of loping steps my way. I coughed, trying to get myself back on my feet before he burned me to a crisp. In my peripheral vision—fuzzy as it was from the lack of oxygen—I watched as his acolytes continued to try and deal with my friends. Taron batted them away from Gethin with ease. For his part, Gethin was snuffing out the lights overhead. As he did so, the temperature continued to drop around us. I could see the strain in Taron's eyes as it affected him.

Hold on. Just a little longer.

The beast looming over me looked unconcerned with being plunged into darkness. He let out another torrent of flames. I braced for the pain, but none came. Instead, Rory positioned herself in front of me with the shield held in both hands. Her feet dug into the gravel underfoot even as the barrage of fire kept coming.

"I can't hold it much longer. You need to do something."

I tried to assess my options. Short of confining them in stone, there was little else we could do. Sure, Taron and Gethin might be able to subdue the rest of his acolytes, but that wouldn't stop Vilmar from continuing his rampage or from spreading his message of hate and bigotry. I'd meant what I'd told Rory. I didn't believe in killing unless we had no other option. Well, it seemed like without taking out Vilmar permanently, the Syndicate would continue to come for us. Sure, maybe they'd survive his death. But we had to try and cut the head off the proverbial snake.

And his own kind had given me the tool to do it. It almost seemed a poor design flaw that a dragon-forged blade could do such damage to the ones who had created it, but maybe it was a way to keep themselves in check. They knew they weren't impervious. Maybe they needed a reminder that they too had an end to their time on this planet. Immortality wasn't all it was cracked up to be when you aren't able to change with the times.

"Vilmar, you were a scholar once," I called, struggling to get to my feet. "Why else would you hold on to so much of that history? You wanted to preserve it, but you got stuck in the past; in a time where you thought dragons knew better. But times change. You can still choose a better way."

'Foolish mortal child.' His voice echoed in my head.

Oh, how I wanted to scream from the mental invasion, but at least I had his attention. He'd stopped trying to burn Rory alive, too. I'd take the win.

"I think we both know how this ends and I don't want that. You have lived a long life, you've seen so much. Surely there are things you could share with the world that would make it better?"

"He's not going to listen," Rory said through gritted teeth.

"I have to try."

'Your pleas fall on deaf ears, girl. You are a minor inconvenience, an annoyance. You will not live long enough to understand that we are immortal. We have existed since the first flame gave birth to our kind.'

"Can't say I didn't give you a chance."

'You would see me confined, weakened, and humiliated.'

"Well, you did try to orchestrate a pointless war and attempted to assassinate the royal family of your own kingdom, so I'd say you're due some confinement."

'*I will never surrender to the likes of you, Morgan Pendragon.*'

"I gave you a chance. What happens next is on you."

I inched forward, my left hand wrapping around Excalibur's hilt. I could feel the blade pulsing with power. I could almost see it planting the thought in my head to strike the dragon's heart. Somehow, I pushed the image out of my mind. If I could simply incapacitate him, sever his connection to the rest of the Syndicate, then Taron's family could bring him to justice. I looked over the edge of the shield and met Taron's gaze. Even in his shifted form I could see the concern in his expression.

'*They will come for him. If he still lives, they will never stop looking for him.*' Taron's words came as if he were speaking them right beside me.

I understood what that took for him to admit. He was losing a piece of his own past, having to face the truth of what Vilmar's true identity meant for him. And he also understood that the creatures in this cave were motivated by vengeance and darkness. I couldn't let that descend onto his kingdom or mine.

'*For our homes, you must do the thing not in your nature.*'

He was giving me permission and somehow, that loosened the knot in my belly. I turned to Rory. "Cover me."

"I'll do what I can." She shifted her grip on the shield and ran toward the dragon, colliding with a meaty thump against his left front leg.

The dragon blew angry puffs of smoke from his nostrils as I darted around his thick torso, searching for the brand that glittered between his wings. I could see damage had already been done, maybe from when I'd nearly confined him at the barrier. Or maybe it was from Taron's assault in the cave a few days earlier. No matter the reason, it was a weak spot, and it drew Excalibur like a homing beacon.

The air around me took on mass, creating stair steps as I bounded upward. I took one last jump and slammed the point of Excalibur's blade into the center of the brand.

I'd never heard such a pained wail as Vilmar's frame shuddered. The brand shattered apart, scales falling to the floor, revealing vulnerable flesh beneath. He thrashed around, trying to reach me, but the confines of the cave worked against him. I knew it wouldn't end his life. I also knew that Excalibur was more than capable of the task.

In one last ditch attempt to end me, Vilmar let out another stream of flames. Somehow, Rory threw herself into the flame, shield held high. The flames sparkled as they struck the gem at the center. To my surprise, the shield not only deflected the attack, but redoubled it back on the dragon. The scent of burning flesh filled the cramped space and I choked as Vilmar's form shrank until he lay burned and naked on the ground. His body twitched as he tried to breathe, but his body refused to let him. I bent over the dying man.

"I truly am sorry it had to come to this."

He rasped and his hands reached out, as if he were going to strangle me. I moved just beyond his reach, only to realize a moment later he wasn't trying to get to me. He had wrapped his hands around Excalibur's blade, drawing blood instantly as his palms dug into the sharp edge. He pulled the blade down until it pierced his chest, slicing through bone and sinew like they were nothing. Blood bubbled on his lips, and he sank to the ground, lifeless.

I looked at the people around me as we all processed his actions to take his own life in the end. The remaining Syndicate members who were still able to move under their own power scurried for any exit they could find. One barely fit past Taron's wing as he continued to hold up the rocks overhead.

"We should go before this whole place comes down around us," Gethin shouted.

I looked at him and then Rory. "You two get out the back. We'll exit the front."

Before Gethin could argue, Rory grabbed him by the wrist and dragged him out the way we'd entered. That left Taron and I standing in the small space, his dragon form taking up every available inch in front of me. I moved to place a hand on the side of his face.

"You were brilliant. But you can let it go now."

A single tear slid down the bronze scales of his face before the wings slowly receded and his mass changed to that of the handsome man I'd met months ago in the lake. I was ready to catch him when he finally stood on two legs again. He rested his head on my shoulder and more tears soaked into my shirt. The rocks around us shifted since he was no longer keeping things secure. I didn't need words to know just how much it had taken from him to stay in dragon form for so long in this world. Somehow, I would find a way to make it up to him. We dashed outside just in time to hear the cave crumble. Dust clouds shot into the night sky as the rock sealed Vilmar's final resting place.

"Let's go home."

TWENTY

I was bone-tired by the time we'd made it back through the barrier into Albion. I was ready to rest, but I knew this quest wasn't finished yet. We still had to find a way to free Laoise from Vilmar's clutches, even if we'd succeeded in taking down the head of the Syndicate of the First Inferno. I also knew the terrorist group wasn't gone for good. Still, I prayed that news of the death of their leader would force them back into hiding for a few centuries.

"We're going to find her," Gethin said, drawing my attention.

I rubbed at the nape of my neck and inhaled slowly. "She's been alone for so long. What if we're too late?"

"You had that vision from her a day ago," Taron

reminded me. "She was alive then. We have no reason to believe anything has changed."

"Sorry to interrupt this very important conversation. But holy shit we were just ... on a hill and now it's a bloody forest." Rory's voice escalated in volume as she spoke.

I smiled in spite of my exhaustion. "It is a bit of a mind fuck the first time you come through," I agreed. "Come on. Let's get to the cave. I believe it will tell us where we're supposed to go next."

"I thought you didn't know where the cave was," Rory noted.

I gestured to the Crystal Cave ahead of us. "Different one. This place is full of them."

She made a 'lead on' gesture and I stepped into the now familiar space, ducking my head to avoid nailing myself on the low-hanging stalactites. The fact I heard Rory give a groan signaled she hadn't taken my cue. I maneuvered to the back of the cave and sat down against the rough wall beside the small pool where so much of this journey had flashed before me.

"Not a ton of space in here," Rory commented as she settled next to me, the shield pressed awkwardly against her torso.

I didn't answer. I just let the cave's stillness

wash over me. I closed my eyes and took several slow breaths, feeling the soil beneath my fingers and listening to the gentle ripples in the water. That still didn't make any sense to me either. There wasn't anywhere for a breeze to come in and yet the water always appeared to have air moving across its surface.

"Are we supposed to—" Rory began, but I held up a finger to quiet her.

Slowly, the world around me slipped away and when I opened my eyes, I found myself in a different cave. Laoise sat in the middle of the room like she'd done every other time I'd seen her. She looked almost peaceful, as if she were just sleeping.

"We made it," I whispered.

My words were enough to make the girl stir. She sat up, her eyes heavy-lidded. "You are coming for me."

"Of course, love. But we don't know how to find you. We've looked where you're meant to be, remember?"

"Wrong time," she murmured, rubbing at her eyes.

What did that mean?

She wasn't in any condition to give me any more

context. I'd have to sort this one out on my own. Wrong time ...

"Oh, I'm so dense." My words echoed painfully in my ears as Laoise's cave vanished, replaced by the one in which Rory and I sat.

My exclamation earned me a quizzical look from Rory. But there wasn't time to explain. I pushed myself to my feet and ran past her, back out into the woods. Gethin and Taron stood shoulder to shoulder just beyond the cave entrance, keeping watch.

"It's been in front of me the whole time and I've missed it."

"Not sure I follow," Rory called, emerging behind me.

"She told me we were looking in the wrong time."

Gethin and Taron's blank stares looked back at me.

"The Tower." I looked at Gethin. "Remember in the Tower of London."

"You got the clue from Gaius," he said slowly.

"But it was like I was really there with him in the past. I stepped through that doorway, and I was in another time."

"You believe Vilmar used a similar spell to keep

the girl hidden just out of reach." Taron caught on fast.

"Makes sense, right? If he knew the shield was powerful, he wouldn't want anyone else to know where to find it. Or that it was forged by a child with extraordinary power. So, he kept her close, but in a way most people wouldn't even think of."

"How would he have known how to do that?" Rory didn't seem fazed by the fact we were talking about the magical equivalent of time travel.

"He's one of the oldest dragons I've known. I wouldn't be surprised if he helped establish the magic. Can you imagine what sort of things the Syndicate could secret away just in a little pocket of history?" Taron's tone was equal parts awe and disgust.

"Hate to point out the flaw in the plan here, but how are we meant to free her?" Gethin adjusted his glasses out of habit.

"We don't know exactly when he caught her and locked her away. It's possible her magic is tied to the shield in more ways than we know. That's got to be the answer," I said.

Marching to the clearing on the Albion side of the trees, I raised my hands and began etching the outline of a circle in the air. I heard three pairs of footsteps thundering through the underbrush behind me.

"Are you certain you can portal us there?" Taron's face carried worry lines that only made him more attractive.

"I will get us there."

Blocking everything else out of my mind, I pictured the artifact room in Vilmar's cave. I imagined myself standing beside the table full of rare bits of Syndicate history. Pieces Vilmar had kept out of fear or maybe even sentimental value. The air was damp, but there was no hint of the poisonous gas he and his ilk were so fond of using. Soon, the tangy taste of limes overwhelmed my sense of smell and taste, beating back the unpleasantness of the cave.

When I opened my eyes, the room sat neatly on the other side of the circle. Maybe it was because we were so close to the end of this journey, but a wave of renewed energy hit me. I could have held the portal open for hours. But we didn't have that long.

"Go on, get through."

Taron led the way, and I caught the way his shoulder muscles tensed the moment he was back in the space. He moved just out of sight, but I could hear the sound of objects moving. Rory and the shield went next, and Gethin brought up the rear. He faltered at the edge of the portal.

"You don't have to go," I assured him.

"I need to see this completed."

His Adam's apple bobbed up and down as he swallowed and stepped through. I followed close behind, letting the portal snap shut behind me. A shiver danced down my spine that had nothing to do with temperature. This place carried a lot of bad memories, and they weren't all mine. What had Laoise managed to see during her captivity? Had he let her out from time to time, taunting her with the thought of freedom?

"This place gives me the creeps," Rory announced and visibly shivered.

"Where did you see her?" Taron paced the perimeter of the space.

I pointed to the wall next to where he'd stopped. He turned to face it and pressed his palms flat against the stone. It appeared rough, but nothing stood out that might reveal a hidden room beyond it. He rapped his knuckles on the stone, moving along the length of the wall. But again, nothing sounded hollow from where I stood. I wish I'd paid more attention at the Tower of London. But I hadn't even realized magic was at play then.

"Hang on a minute, everyone back away from the wall."

Without a word, my three companions took a few steps away. I rounded the empty table in the center of the room and approached the blank wall. I held my hands out as Taron had done, except I didn't touch the stone. I summoned just a bit of my power, putting it out in the space around me, searching for anything that might be actively concealing the room's entrance. The sensation of bumping against something prickly danced across my fingertips and I fought to keep my hands stationary. Yes, there was definitely some sort of spell here. I couldn't say for certain Vilmar cast it, but if he'd done so while he was alive, shouldn't it have sputtered out once he died?

Let me see the spell.

My vision dimmed for a moment before sharpening and I could see tiny angry red lines branching out from the center of the wall. They crisscrossed the length of the wall from floor to ceiling. It almost looked like a spider's web except every strand looked poised to draw blood. But I could sense it was obscuring something. I traced the overlapping lines, trying to find the origin point, but it seemed they just materialized out of nowhere. Trying to tug one or two strands free didn't guarantee success.

"Whoah," Rory said, stepping up beside me. "Do you see this?"

I blinked and faced her. "You can see it?"

"It's like that time Gran tried to knit a sweater. It was all chaos and knotted yarn. Couldn't tell where the strings ended or began."

If this quest had taught me anything, it was that building bonds with my newfound friends was the key. "So, we do it together. I'll start at that end, and you start over there. We'll meet in the middle."

Rory gave me a nod and I watched her fingers deftly moving, as if she were actually unraveling misbehaving yarn from a crafter's bin. I expected the spell to fight back, or at least for it leave a mark on her hands, but it didn't touch her. It was then that I noticed her fingers carried a slight green aura. The shield sat on the table behind us, but the emerald at its heart blazed bright and strong. I tried my hand at dismantling a piece of the spell on my end. Its barbs receded the moment I got close enough. A hazy blue light emanated from my fingertips that I had to assume was thanks to Excalibur.

The thin red veins of magic faded altogether the moment mine and Rory's hands touched the center of the wall. The room shook with bits of dust and loose rocks cascading from overhead. I waited for the shaking to stop, but it only intensified the longer we stood there.

"I think whatever you just did triggered some sort of self-destruct sequence," Gethin said, his voice strained.

"Brilliant," I groaned as the rockface in front of me cracked and a small depression appeared. It looked about the size of the emerald in the shield.

Before I could speak, Rory pivoted and grabbed the shield. Gently, she plucked the gem from the center of the metal. I watched as the metal, battered as it was, knit itself back together to fill the space where the stone had been. Filing that curiosity away for another time, I watched as Rory pressed the emerald into the space within the rock. The wall gave a cacophonous groan as it shifted, receding into itself until there was space enough for an average sized adult to walk through. Laoise lay on the harsh stone floor, eyes closed. I rushed in as the floor continued to shake.

"Hi there. We've got you," I said as gently as I could while still trying to rouse her.

She opened her eyes, looked up at me and smiled. "I knew you would find me."

"We need to go, now." Taron's voice echoed in the artifact room. I scooped the girl into my arms and took off at a sprint. I looked back just long enough to see Rory retrieve both the shield and emerald before taking off. Gethin and Taron were ahead of us, leading the way out of the cavern and into the fresh air. I turned back just in time to hear a concussive 'boom' fill the air. The cave collapsed in on itself, burying everything in a heavy layer of rubble and mountain debris.

"Well, that's one way to cripple their operation," I said with a smirk.

"Not that almost dying again isn't really exciting, but I am ready to go home," Gethin announced.

"Me, too, mate."

The burst of energy that had gotten us here was starting to fade. Still, I had promised to get everyone home and I intended to keep my word. I handed Laoise to Rory and started to trace another circle in the air when a familiar voice called my name.

"Morgan, you don't do things by halves, do you?" Talia appeared from around the edge of the mountain.

"Suppose not. Please tell me you have a very convenient way back to Camelot that doesn't involve magical burnout."

"Indeed, we do." Emerys appeared behind the dragon princess and the look of pure relief on her face made me want to collapse.

In short order, she'd portaled Gethin, Rory, Laoise, and I back to Camelot, leaving Taron and Talia to make their own way home. But there were still questions that needed answers. How long ago had Vilmar taken Laoise? Did she have any family left to miss her? Even if she had no blood relatives left, there was no way in hell I was going to let her be alone again.

As we settled back in at the castle, I let out a breath I'd been holding for weeks. The Syndicate of the First Inferno would hopefully limp off into obscurity for a while and maybe, just maybe, things would settle down.

A QUICK AUTHOR'S NOTE

COMING INTO THIS BOOK, I'll admit I didn't have quite as much of a solid plan for what was about to happen. I knew, following on from the discovery at the end of Her Amethyst Pendant, that we'd be spending time with the dragons and Taron specifically. But I hadn't anticipated the link he'd have to the Syndicate or how that might affect his burgeoning relationship with Morgan. And I found myself feeling the character's aggravation as they tried to have little romantic moments and they just getting foiled. There was a point in time as I was writing this that I had a certain plot point in mind and it turned out that it became a major stumbling block for me, holding me up for a good week as I tried to figure out how it was going to fit. As it turns out, my initial thought that Morgan and Taron would get to consummate their relationship in this book did not in fact fit where the plot wound up going. So, it got pushed (don't worry, it's not been wholly abandoned).

I also had general thoughts of how this book might also tie more directly into the Seasons verse with the character of Professor Nobles. When we first met him in the original series, he was rather cocky and a bit of an dick. But I liked this idea of getting to revisit him a bit later and see if he'd mended his ways. As it turns out, only slightly. But I appreciated getting to make those connections again.

When I sat down to plan the series, I knew that each book (at least for a while) would follow a similar trajectory of having to track down a magical item and connect with a new ally. But I found it kind of refreshing that the hunt for the shield in this book didn't happen right away. We got to explore some other characters and forge those relationships and I have to admit I loved getting to see Talia again. I have a feeling she and Gethin are going to be fast friends after she saved his life. Then again, it almost felt like there could have been something brewing with Rory, too. Only time will tell.

I did feel a little sad with the limited appearances by some of our other characters, but with an ever-expanding circle of powerful women, sometimes you have to pick and choose who gets the spotlight. Besides, it makes for a great opportunity for some little side quests down the line. Speaking of expanding Morgan's circle, I had a very strong idea of what Book 5 would be and I think you're going to really enjoy it. We get to revisit the Seelies and some pieces of Morgan's history not even she is fully aware of.

Turn the page for a glimpse at Her Obsidian Bow...

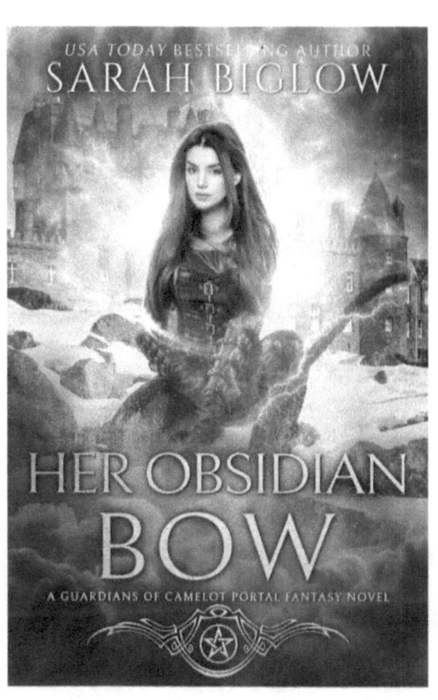

Sometimes the strongest bonds are forged in tragedy...

Morgan le Fey is ready to fully embrace her status as Camelot's future Queen, even agreeing to a sit-down interview so her subjects can get to know the real her. But when the attempt ends in embarrassment, she fears she's done more to harm her reputation than bolster it. Still, she's ready to shrug it off and pretend it never happened until a terrifying vision sends her on another quest into the heart of enemy territory.

She must recover an ancient obsidian bow, put on display in the seelie throne room, without anyone being the wiser. Going undercover seems the only option, but one wrong step could see her imprisoned or worse, dead.

She'll have to rely on her burgeoning relationship with Prince Taron and his retinue to keep her secret and formulate a plan to steal the bow and make it out before anyone finds out. All seems set to go off without a hitch, until a young Seelie woman with a harrowing connection to Morgan uncovers their plan. Can Morgan convince her that aiding her kingdom's enemy is the only way to earn her freedom, or will decades of resentment and betrayal doom Morgan's efforts for good?

Scan the QR code to get your copy of Her Obsidian Bow.

ABOUT THE AUTHOR

Sarah Biglow is a *USA Today* bestselling author. She lives in Massachusetts with her husband and son. She is a licensed attorney and spends her days combatting employment discrimination as an Investigator with the Massachusetts Commission Against Discrimination.

You can find an up-to-date list of all my books here